THE VEGAS PITCH

AMANDA SHELLEY

Visit my website at
www.amandashelley.com

CONNECT WITH AMANDA SHELLEY

Want to be the first to know about upcoming sales and new releases? Make sure you sign up for my newsletter as well as connect with me on social media and your favorite retail store.

Website:
www.amandashelley.com
Newsletter:
https://geni.us/AmandaShelleyNL
Facebook:
https://www.facebook.com/authoramandashelley/
Instagram:
https://www.instagram.com/authoramandashelley/
Reader's Group:
https://www.facebook.com/groups/AmandasArmyofReaders/
Tik Tok:
https://www.tiktok.com/@authoramandashelley
Amazon:
https://www.amazon.com/author/amandashelley
Goodreads:
https://www.goodreads.com/author/show/19713563.Amanda_Shelley

Book Bub:

https://www.bookbub.com/profile/amanda-shelley

The Vegas Pitch
By Amanda Shelley

This pitch could make or break my career.

Not only will it set a personal record for the biggest account I've ever landed, but it could set my newfound company three years ahead of schedule for expansion.

Thank God I've got Nate Bellinger on my team.

Even though I had my reservations hiring the sexiest man I've ever laid eyes on—he more than meets my expectations with his hard work and determination. Together, we've formed a solid team and play off each other perfectly.

As we wait for the final verdict, I begrudgingly take Nate up on his offer for a night on the town. After all, this is Vegas, and I need to let the chips fall where they may.

Imagine my surprise when I wake up the next morning to find we've not only won the campaign, but I'm apparently married to the man I've only ever let myself fantasize about.

The kicker of it all—he has no intentions of letting me go.

But what will it mean once we leave Vegas?

Chapter 1

Annie

BUZZ... buzzzz... buzzzzzz.

Make it stop... just make it stop.

Buzz... buzzzz... buzzzzzz.

Wait? Is that my phone?

Buzz... buzzzz... buzzzzzz.

Oh, shit, it is.

Scrambling across the bed, I fumble for the offensive noise this early in the morning.

Seeing my biggest potential client's name illuminate the screen, I'm suddenly on high alert as I frantically swipe at the call, hoping like hell I can answer before it goes to voice mail.

"Hel...Hello?" comes out breathless.

A woman's crisp tone comes through the line. "Ms. Holstings?"

"This is she." Closing my eyes, I hold my breath as I wait for more.

"My name is Riley Bennett. I'm Mr. Worthington's personal secretary."

Instantly, my shoulders sag, and I'm certain she's about to deliver terrible news.

Mr. Worthington said he himself would reach out if we won the contract. My blood turns to ice as what's riding on this news flashes through my mind.

I've put my life on hold, bending over backward for the past six months to land this account. The Worthington is one of the biggest hotels being constructed on The Strip, and a client like this, with multiple destinations around the world, could've put my advertising firm three years ahead of schedule —in terms of expansion.

Christ. I was really counting on this, and thought my chances were good.

As I mentally roam down the road of despair, the lady on the other end continues, as if she isn't about to rip my dreams to shreds. "He wants me to relay a message to you as soon as possible."

"Okay..." I draw out, sinking onto my pillow, hoping she'll put me out of my misery sooner than later.

"Mr. Worthington sends his deepest regrets he couldn't do this in person, but a family emergency has pulled him away."

"I'm sorry to hear that," I manage to spit out, as my stomach drops to the floor, waiting for the proverbial shoe to drop.

The woman on the other end takes in a deep breath. "Yes. It is rather unfortunate...but as I was saying, he'd like me to relay a message..."

Oh, for the love of God, just say it already.

I hear papers wrestling on her end of the phone, and I seriously want to reach my hand through the line and strangle her for making me wait any longer. This is pure agony, knowing my dreams are about to be ripped away.

"Here it is. Sorry about that. I needed to check my notes to talk about the specifics of what Mr. Worthington wished to convey himself. He said, and I quote, 'Your firm is exactly what Worthington Industries is looking for. You're young, fresh, and have your thumb on the pulse of what people expect for a new expansion as grand as this.' He'd like you to return to Vegas on the twenty-eighth, to tour the construction site, so you can get a feel for exactly the space and the layout for your grand opening campaign."

Holy shit. This is unexpected.

Pumping my fist in the air, I do a little happy dance in the bed and silently scream my excitement.

"Ms. Holstings? Are you there?"

"Yes," I quickly assure her. "Yes, we'll be there."

"Since this is short notice, Mr. Worthington asked if I could make travel arrangements for you—and any member of your team you deem necessary, from Seattle to Las Vegas."

Somehow, my wits return, and I manage to sound calm as I interject. "That won't be necessary."

"Ma'am, he insists on making one of the company's jets available that day. He only has a small window of availability. He'd like to use the flight as an opportunity to finish the final details before you tour the site together."

A private jet? To Vegas?

"Well, when you put it that way, I'm happy to let you make the arrangements." I concede. If Mr. Worthington wants to use the flight to conduct business, it will be far more effective if we took his jet. "It will just be Mr. Bellinger and myself traveling that day."

"Great. The jet typically flies out of Paine Field, to avoid traffic at Sea-Tac. Will you need help in getting arrangements to the airport?"

"No. That won't be necessary."

She prattles on but assures me she'll email the details as well, so I don't bother looking for a pen to write the specifics. The poor woman on the other side has no clue how little I'm paying attention at this point because I'm still reeling over the fact that our pitch won us this account.

I mean, I knew Holstings' Creative had a real shot. We were on point with our research and marketing analysis. We know Worthington Industries inside and out. But we're still small—in terms of advertising firms, and we knew it would be a long shot against other major conglomerates.

But we did it... we fucking did it! Nate and I went in there yesterday and kicked ass. It takes everything in my power to listen to the things Riley continues to prattle about. When she finally ends the call with, "If you need anything, please don't hesitate to reach out." I can barely contain myself.

The moment I end the call and place my phone back on the nightstand, two warm arms snake around my torso, and a warm breath nuzzles into my neck. My entire body stiffens when I realize two things simultaneously—first, I'm not alone, and second, I'm completely naked, and so is the man behind me.

What the hell happened last night?

Before I can process this information, a low moan comes

from the man as he kisses my neck. "Hmmmm... it looks like we have one more thing to celebrate."

Holy fucking shit. I'd recognize that sexy voice in my sleep. Hell, I've dreamed about this man, but I have never in my wildest desires let myself go there.

Goose bumps erupt all over my flesh as kisses feather along my shoulder. Hmmm. It's hard to think, as I assess the situation and replay the events of the last few minutes in my head.

This feels too good to be true, and my brain disconnects, succumbing to the sensation. Closing my eyes, I enjoy the fantasy coming to life as hot kisses pepper my neck and shoulders, and warm hands roam my body, holding me in place. My body lights on fire when he cups my breast and thumbs across my nipple as the other hand flows south and cups my mound. The moment a finger strokes my clit, I'm convinced there's only one explanation to the events in this moment.

I must be dreaming.

And as I'm on the precipice to a ginormous release, there's no way I'm waking.

Nope, Nate Bellinger is one of my biggest fantasies come true. He's the man I've often let myself picture when I need to take the edge off and take matters into my own hand. Not only is he tall, handsome, and sexy as sin. He's also wicked smart and extremely talented—and someone who's completely off limits—as he's an employee. Hence, the reason why I only allow myself to fantasize about this man.

Fuck, I've never had a dream so vivid in my life.

It's like I'm climbing to the top of a rollercoaster, teetering on the edge of exploding, and my entire body trembles.

Chasing the impending orgasm, I feel his grip on my body tighten as sparks of energy explode everywhere in an instant. "Oh my God, best dream ever," I pant as pulse after pulse rocks through my body.

I'm brought back to reality when Nate hauls me into his arm and chuckles. "Not a dream, wife," he says, coaxing me to my back, so he can eagerly crawl up my body.

The way his heated eyes pin mine, I gulp audibly, as I process his words.

"Not. A. Dream. Wife?"

What the hell? There's no way I'd dream of something this vivid.

When he reaches for my left hand and kisses my knuckles, I notice something that's never been there before.

A ring.

Not just any ring, a white gold or platinum band with a huge round diamond shining back at me.

As events from the last twenty-four hours rush back at me, my mind whirls with wonder.

What the hell have I gotten myself into?

Chapter 2

Annie

"…And this is why we believe Holstings' Creative will make the launch of The Worthington the talk of the town. People will flock to Vegas to experience all The Worthington has to offer."

As I look around the boardroom, I'm greeted with curt smiles and nods. It's Mr. Worthington who breaks the silence. "Thank you for your time, Ms. Holstings. I'll be in touch personally, to let you know our decision in the next few days."

Well, that's something, isn't it?

He nods to his fellow colleagues, and our meeting disassembles.

As the room empties, Mr. Worthington walks to Nate and me to shake our hands and personally thanks us for our time and effort put into this project thus far.

"If you have any further questions, please don't hesitate to reach out," I say as he releases my hand.

"Will. Do." Mr. Worthington nods, then exits the room with his peers.

The moment Nate and I are alone, I turn to him nervously and ask, "What do you think?"

Nodding, he grins. "Personally, I think we left it all on the table, and if we're the best fit for them, they'll choose us."

"Hmmmm…" I grumble, not sure how I feel about his assessment. I mean, we could have said a few things differently. I'm certainly not sure how the VP felt because that man had a poker face from the moment we walked in. On autopilot, I pack my laptop and gather our things, replaying the entire presentation in my mind.

Just when I've packed the last of my things, Nate reaches out and grips my wrist. I ignore the bolt of electricity that zings through me each and every time we touch and do my best to focus on his face as I ask, "What?"

"You and I are going out tonight," he demands. His expression leaves little room for argument.

"We are?" I ask, holding my chin high, trying like hell not to show how his touch impacts me.

"Yes. I know you, Annabelle Holstings. Better than you think." He takes a deep breath and exhales slowly as he pins me with those amber eyes I often find myself lost in. "You'll go back to your room, get stuck in your head, and worry yourself sick over the possible outcome. That is *not* happening tonight."

"You got a better plan?" I challenge.

"Yep." He nods triumphantly. "And it starts with dinner."

Starts? There's a glimmer of mischief in his expression I've never seen before. It's intriguing, and I'm half-tempted to give in, just to see where it leads.

Before I can come back with anything witty, he smirks. "When was the last time you ate?"

Oh, hell. How am I supposed to remember that? I was too nervous to eat this morning.

"That's what I thought. First dinner, then our goal is to get your mind off this pitch. You and I both know what we have riding on this."

"Don't remind me," I groan. The entire future of my company I've worked to build from the ground up is riding on this.

"That's my point. We've done all we can to earn this account. We've left our hearts in this room. But I'll be damned if we're leaving our minds. Tonight, we're living in the moment. Throwing our worries to the wind and only focusing on the right here and now."

This look right here. The one filled with sheer determination is why I brought Nate on board with me the moment I could afford to expand Holstings' Creative. He'd worked with me at Meyer & Cross, and I've seen him completely take charge of a boardroom. He doesn't take no for an answer, and his gut instinct is usually spot on.

Which of course—he is, whether or not I want to admit it.

"Okay... okay..." I grumble when I realize he's made his point. "What's for dinner?"

"First, let's go back to our room and change into something less formal and get ready for a night out on the town in celebration."

"Uh, don't ya think you're putting the cart before the horse?"

Shaking his head curtly, he grins. "Nope. We're celebrating the fact that we gave it our best shot. We can finally relax because the chips will fall where they may, and there's absolutely nothing we can do at this point. So, let's celebrate the efforts we've put into this project. No matter the outcome—we should both be proud of the pitch we've spent countless hours preparing."

"Are you sure this won't jinx us?" I worry.

"We're not celebrating the win. We're celebrating that we can *finally* relax and know no matter what, we've given it our all. No sense in stressing out more."

Well, when he puts it that way...

"Okay... okay. Point taken," I concede. "But you gotta give me something on what to wear if we're getting out of business attire."

"My brother has an in with one of the hottest clubs on the strip. He's put my name on the list for dinner. So, what do you say, Annie? You wanna paint the town red tonight?"

Nate's brother, Nash, is the kicker for the Rainier Renegades. He was recently drafted, and it's not hard to believe a professional athlete would have connections. The thought of letting loose in one of the hottest clubs on the strip does sound enticing. Ever since I ventured out on my own, I've been all work and no play. A night out will be good for me.

Besides, Nate's with me. What's the worst that could happen?

Decision made; I grin.

"Okay. You've got a deal," I say, reaching out my hand to shake.

Nate's grin almost leaves me breathless. "On one condition…"

Hesitantly, I ask, "What's that?"

"We're both open to a night of firsts. We've both been working our asses off, and it's time we let down our walls and just have fun."

"HERE'S TO HAVING FUN!" I shout above the crowd and music, then swig down my second Kamikaze shot.

As Nate and I both slam the shot glass down on the high-top table in front of us, he grins triumphantly. "I never thought I'd see the day when Annabelle Holstings is out on the town with me."

"Well… you know." I grin as my hips sway to the music in the club. "What happens in Vegas…"

Leaning in so only I can hear, his warm breath sends shivers throughout my body. "I'm gonna hold you to that, Annie."

I love when he calls me Annie. Only my close friends and family are allowed, but somehow when he says it, it sends shivers to all the right places. Maybe that's why the moment he reaches for my hand to pull me onto the dance floor, I follow him without hesitation.

The dance floor is crowded and the moment we reach his destination, he draws me close. At first, I hesitate. But the delicious scent of his cologne and his playful smirk has me throwing caution to the wind and looping my arms around his neck as our bodies sway to the beat.

His body against mine feels amazing.

When Nate's muscular thigh slides between my legs, I've never been more thankful for my best friend Teagan. Especially when the skirt of my little black dress she insisted I pack slips further up my thighs. Simultaneously, as his thigh slips further, his hand grips my hip, pulling me closer as his eyes roam my body, making me feel as if I'm the sexiest woman in the room. I'd chosen to wear a flirty A-line dress with an empire waist and halter top. My back is bare, and the moment he trails his other hand along my spine, goose bumps erupt along my flesh, even though it's warm on the dance floor.

Leaning in so I can hear his deep voice, he says, "I like this side of you."

How can that alone make my panties melt?

My muscles clench in an effort to hide my arousal, as I admit, "I haven't let loose like this in... forever." Well, ever if I'm being honest. But now that I've finally allowed myself to be this close to him, I'm in no hurry to leave the dance floor. Because then I'd have to let go.

The music changes to a fast song I don't recognize, but the crowd around us buzzes with energy in recognition. The volume of the dance floor suddenly amplifies, essentially ending all opportunities for conversation.

As much as I'll miss not hearing his rough, sexy voice in my ear, I know if we'd kept up our conversation, I'd eventually get stuck in my head. Instead, I finally do what I'd promised

Nate earlier. I close my eyes and allow myself to be lost in this moment.

The pulse of the music flows through my body as I breathe in Nate's delicious scent. It's rich and masculine, almost like top-shelf bourbon with a bit of oak, musk, and something entirely Nate. I'm not sure which has a greater effect, him or the alcohol flowing through my system. Frankly, I don't care. I just want more of Nate.

One song turns into the next, and we stay on the dance floor. Eventually, we're both thirsty and out of breath, so we break apart. With the crowded room, Nate reaches for my hand as if it's the most natural thing in the world and leads me to our table where a waitress quickly arrives. He orders a Seven and Seven for himself, and I choose a Kamikaze cocktail.

Once our waitress leaves, Nate leans over the table and raises a brow as he asks, "What's something you've never done in Vegas?"

"Hmmm..." I draw out, wondering what on earth I'd like to do. "I've only come here for work, so basically anything touristy."

"You've never come here for fun?" he asks in disbelief, and I shake my head

"Well, I'm glad we're changing that tonight," he says before taking his drink from the waitress. "Thanks."

"Anything else I can get you?" she asks us as she places my drink on the table.

Nate quickly looks at me, and I shake my head, and he replies, "We're good, thanks."

"So..." Nate says as he reaches for his drink, his expression unreadable. "How are we gonna fix this?"

Confused, I sputter, "Fix... what?"

"This all work and no play Annabelle."

"I play..." *God, could I sound more like a petulant child?*

He's quiet as he takes another drink. "When was the last time you did anything spontaneous?"

"I'm here, aren't I?" I hedge and take a long, fortifying drink from my straw.

Nate holds my gaze and nods once in agreement. But clearly, he's not satisfied. The arch of his brow is all I need as a challenge. I make a split-second decision to finish the rest of my drink right then and there. The moment my straw slurps, I jump to my feet and reach for his hand.

A light laugh escapes as he rises to his feet. "God, I love this side of you." is all that's needed to spur me on.

Effortlessly, I drag him to the dance floor. Within seconds, I loop my arms around his neck and as his hand comes to my hip, we move with the beat. I love how I feel with Nate. I'm tired of overthinking things, and I'm ready to get lost in him again.

"LET'S stop to watch the fountain," Nate suggests, pulling me up to the railing. Somehow, we managed to snag a spot dead center for the show. Who knows how long we'll have to wait, but as long as Nate's beside me, I'm not complaining.

Ever since we left the dance floor, Nate's hands have been

on me in one way or another. Whether it's how he guides me by the base of my back, grabbing my hand as we weave through the crowded strip, or leaning in against me from behind as he wraps an arm around my waist to hold me close while we wait for the famous show at the fountain to begin. Nate's touch feels incredible. I keep getting caught off guard by the shivers zinging along my spine when his skin comes into contact with mine.

You'd think I'd be used to it by the amount of contact we've had this evening, but that's hardly the case. Each and every time, my belly flips, and my senses overload. The distinct scent of his cologne continues to intoxicate me, just as much as the alcohol I've consumed. Honestly, I'm not sure which is more powerful and frankly, I no longer care. Especially when he brushes a loose strand of hair from my face and hypnotizes me with his gorgeous eyes and sexy smile.

God, those lips.

I'd be a self-made millionaire if I got a dollar for each and every time I've wanted to kiss that smirk off his face.

"What's going on in that beautiful head of yours, Annie?"

Oh, hell. Did he have to choose this moment to pay attention to my ogling?

Leaning in so only I can hear, he whispers in my ear, "You've got to tell me what's suddenly made you—the queen of the boardroom—the woman who's never shy—suddenly blush about fifty shades of red."

Fifty shades... why'd he have to go *there*?

I feel him pull back, and his warmth disappears, as his hands grip my hips, spinning me to face him. Leaning in so we're practically eye to eye, Nate pointedly reminds me, "You promised you'd stay out of your head, Annie. Tell me what's going on."

He's so close, his warm breath washes over my face, and my eyes lock on his lips once again before I force myself to meet his heated gaze.

His hand reaches out to cup my cheek and instinctively, I lean into his touch.

"Annie?"

"Yes?" comes out breathless as I get lost in his eyes, and I find myself leaning even closer. We're barely a breath apart. I can't believe he expects me to think at a time like this.

Thankfully, I don't have to because the next thing I know, his lips crash onto mine. I swear I hear fireworks. Or maybe it's just my thudding heart hammering against my chest as his kiss completely consumes me. The moment his tongue sweeps out, my lips part with ease, inviting him in.

His kiss is possessive and all consuming. The world around us disappears, and all I know is I want more.

This is so much better than I could ever imagine.

Gripping his shirt, I pull him closer as the hand at my neck tilts my head, allowing our kiss to deepen. I'm faintly aware of music starting around me as well as the sound of oohs and aahs, but maybe it's just my mind exploding in pleasure. I mean, Nate Bellinger is kissing me. I've always had a vivid imagination, but even my wildest fantasies about this man pale in comparison to the real deal.

We pull apart breathless and panting. I'll never forget how

his lips pull into a devilish grin and the heated gaze that could detonate my panties in a millisecond.

Running a thumb across my swollen lips, he practically growls, "You have no idea how long I've been wanting to do that."

What? He's been wanting to kiss me, too?

As I process his words, he grins even wider.

Before I can respond, the fountain explodes like crazy, and we're distracted by the suddenly louder music and the water dancing in patterns across the entire property. We take a moment to watch the rest of the show. We must've missed more than I thought because I'm fairly certain we're catching the grand finale.

As Frank Sinatra croons "Fly Me To The Moon", Nate steps behind me, wraps his arms around me, and sways to the music. My heart nearly melts when he sings the lyrics in my ear, right along with Ol' Blue Eyes. Holy shit, Sinatra has a fantastic voice, but so does Nate.

This is certainly a side of him I never expected.

Electric pulses run rampant throughout my body as we sway to the jazzy beat. As much as I'm dying to say something, I keep my lips glued shut, in fear of Nate stopping. Each and every lyric both Nate and Frank sing hits my heart and makes me wish those words could be true.

Especially the last three.

As Nate punctuates, "I. Love. You." he leans in and kisses my neck. If he weren't holding me up, I'm sure I'd be a puddle of goo on this sidewalk. A girl can only dream of a man as sexy as Nate serenading her like this.

How am I supposed to handle reality?

When the song ends, I close my eyes and bask in the moment. There's no way I want to be the one to pop this incredible bubble we've built around us.

When his grip around me tightens, he leans in and whispers, "You okay, Annie?"

"More than okay," I admit, but I'm fearful of turning around to realize I'm entirely stuck in my head, and this means nothing to him.

Eventually, people walk away from the fountain, and I'm forced to face reality. Slowly, I turn around, schooling my features so I won't show my disappointment if his expression doesn't mirror my feelings.

My worries are quickly put at ease when I see his sexy smile and his heated expression has returned. Without a word, he leans in and kisses the hell out of me once again.

This time when we break apart, he reaches for my hand. "Fair warning, now that I've had a taste, I'm nowhere finished with you."

My body screams, *Oh, God, yes. I'm not done with you either.*

But my brain kicks in at that exact moment, and I sputter, "But... I'm... your boss..."

His lips purse for a moment before he draws out, "I'm well aware of that. But we're both adults."

"True. But... what will happen if things end badly? I can't afford to lose you," I sputter once again. Not only is he a valuable employee, but since it's essentially just the two of us, he's become a close friend, too.

As my mind reels with all the reasons we shouldn't be together, he squeezes my hand and asks, "But what if it doesn't end?"

"Wait... what... What did you just say?"

"Who says this has to end, Annabelle?"

"Uh... don't most relationships?" I hedge, facing the only reality I've ever known. I mean all my relationships have. My parents were divorced before I was six, and my grandma was a widow, and I never met my grandfather. Obviously, relationships are bound to end in one way or another.

"They don't have to," he points out and steps closer to me. "You promised you'd stay out of your head tonight."

"But you just threw me a curve ball," I spit out on a laugh. "How can you expect me *not* to be in my head?"

"Look, I know you don't do casual relationships. What will it take to get you to realize I'm in this for the long haul? I've liked you since... hell, practically since the day we met, I've been attracted to you. I admire your strength, your tenacity, and your balls to go out on your own to follow your dreams. Why the hell do you think I followed you from Meyer & Cross?"

"Uh, because I gave you a competitive wage?"

"Oh... you beautiful, smart, and silly woman. I followed you because I believe in you. The more I got to know you, the more I fell for you. At first, I was playing the field and dating regularly. But the more we worked together, the more I realized I was comparing everyone else to you. So about six months ago, I said fuck it—I'm holding out for you. I can't be with anyone else when you're all I think about. Why else do you think I took every opportunity to spend more time together?"

I'm sure he means it as a rhetorical question, but of course, I open my big mouth and answer him, "I thought you were dedicated to the job and wanted Holstings' Creative to succeed."

"I do. Never doubt that."

"But..." I interrupt. Is he really saying what I think he's saying? God, this is not the time to not be firing on all cylinders, Annie. Get it together.

"But nothing. If you don't feel the same, I can respect that."

"I do," I blurt out, and I cringe when I see his brows knit with confusion.

"Do what?" he draws out slowly.

Fuck. What do I mean? Where do I even start? Hell. Just say it, Annie. Sucking in a quick breath, I blurt out, "I like you, too."

A triumphant grin I've seen plenty of times when he's helped us win accounts spreads over his face, and he closes the gap between us. "I'm so fucking happy to hear you say that." Those are the last words I hear before his sensual lips crash onto mine.

I'm not sure how long we kiss. It could be minutes, hours, or days. This time when he kisses me, it's different. Somehow knowing he feels the same way about me makes me want him even more.

When we pull apart, he brushes a stray hair from my face and grins. "Are we good?" he asks.

Me being me, my brain whirls, and my contingency plans kick in. "I'm good... but what happens if..."

Placing a finger over my lips, he says, "Stop. Get out of your head. Just feel."

"But..." I start, and he cuts me off again.

"What's it gonna take for you to realize I'm in this for the long haul?"

Holy shit. He's serious.

"But I'm your boss... you're my employee." I point out the biggest obstacle standing in my way.

His brows raise. "Do I need to quit?"

Crap. "No. Please don't. That's exactly what I'm afraid of..." I trail off, biting my lip, hoping it won't come to that. I may like him, but I'd be sunk without him, especially if we land the Worthington account.

His lips purse, and he looks to the sky, like I've seen him do countless times when his wheels are spinning, and he's formulating his next move. I can tell the second he's made his decision. His eyes lock on mine, and a victorious grin spreads across his face.

Instead of filling me in on his plan, he slowly runs his tongue along his lower lip like a sly fox, as he stares into my eyes. "I meant what I said. I'm in this for the long haul. What if..." he says, reaching for my hand and giving it a squeeze.

"What if... instead of being your employee, I held another role..."

Trying to read his mind, I spit out, "Partner?"

"Of sorts..." he draws out. "I'm glad we're on the same

page. What if instead of being merely an employee... I was your partner in everything!"

Before I can process what he means, he drops to the ground. His eyes never leave mine when he clears his throat and continues. "I want to be your partner in the boardroom and in all aspects of your life. I meant it, Annie, when I said I'm in this for the long haul. What if I was your husband? What do you say, Annabelle Marie Holstings, will you be my wife?"

All the air escapes my lungs as I stare at the beautiful man before me.

Did he just drop to one knee and propose?

When I don't say anything, he squeezes my hands to break me from my revelry. "You promised you'd stay out of your head tonight. Talk to me. Tell me what you're thinking?"

My eyes roam from his hands back to his gorgeous eyes as a million thoughts freefall through my mind. But the moment my eyes meet his, I know there's only one answer to his question. Throwing caution to the wind, I nod once.

His head quirks to the side. "I'm gonna need words, Annie."

"Yes." That just might be the most spontaneous thing I've ever said.

Jumping up from the ground, his lips crash onto mine, and I vow to stay in the moment and simply experience all that is Nate.

Chapter 3

Nate

MAKING Annie come is hands down my favorite way to start the morning. Being with her is better than a dream come true. We made love all through the night and waking up with her receiving the news that's had her on pins and needles for weeks, just makes it even better. Now we have even more to celebrate. Not only is she finally with me, but we've just landed the biggest account of both of our lives. We've spent countless hours working on this pitch, and I'm beyond excited to know all our hard work has paid off.

After learning Annie's body last night, I didn't think things could get any better. I certainly didn't come to Vegas expecting to be married. Hell, I didn't even know if I'd get the opportunity to tell her how I feel. Even though it's hands down the most spontaneous thing I've ever done, I have zero regrets.

I've been comparing everyone to her for ages. She's it for me. It was just a matter of time before I broke down and finally told her.

I know with the way we ran with the moment last night, we'll have plenty of details to work out... later. But right now, I need to make love to her more than I need my next breath.

"Wife..." she whispers, looking down at the ring I splurged

for last night. There's no way we were getting married with simple bands. That just wouldn't do. My proposal may have been on a whim, but Annie still deserves the best.

While she had slipped into a department store in our hotel to change into a white dress, I popped into a jewelry store and purchased a ring worthy of her. It was almost closing, but they had no problem staying open to make another happy customer.

I'm so happy I had sprung for the video and pictures of our ceremony because even though I'll never forget the look on her face when I slid this ring on her finger, I'm glad we're able to preserve the memory all the same.

Looking at me with awe, she whispers, "Am I really your wife?"

"According to the state of Nevada, you are," I tease.

"I... uh... don't think I've ever been more spontaneous," she murmurs, biting on her lip.

Shit. She's gonna get in her head and overthink the hell out of this.

Reaching for her face, I tip it to look at mine. "I meant what I said last night. I want to be with you in the boardroom, the bedroom, and everywhere in between. I know this is a huge step—for both of us. I may not have planned it, but it doesn't mean I don't want it."

"Nate, we didn't just fall into bed last night—which on its own would've been a big deal—because I've liked you forever —but we eloped."

Remembering how gorgeous she looked walking down the aisle, I smile at the memory. "Yes, we did. My feelings for you aren't gonna change, Annie. If we're gonna give it a go, why not go all in? It's not fair to either of us if we only go halfway. No relationship ever works if you're both not one hundred percent in this."

She pinches up her nose and squints at me. "Would you stop... being... so perfect?"

I can't help it, I laugh. She's adorable.

"Oh, trust me, I'm far from perfect. I've got flaws, as I'm sure you do, as well—but I'm committed to see where this goes, aren't you?"

"Nate... if you only knew how much I've wanted you over the years... but don't ya think we jumped the gun... just a little?"

"With anyone else, I would absolutely agree with you. But this is us. You know me better than most of my family. We've spent countless hours for the better part of a year together. We have the same goals and aspirations for life. We both get stuck inside our head and overthink things to death. We've been colleagues, even though you've been my boss, I'd like to think we've become friends, too."

"But what will this mean for my company?" she gasps.

"It's still your company; I'm happy to sign anything necessary to give you that piece of mind. We've talked about me becoming a partner and owning a certain percentage if we were to expand it the way you've always dreamed of. That can still happen or not. I'm not willing to lose you now that I've just got you. You can still be the boss in the boardroom, just so you know that won't always be the case in *our* bedroom," I tack on with a sly grin.

God, I feel like our pitch yesterday has nothing in terms of the stakes riding on this conversation. I know I'm laying it on thick, but I'm not about to let everything I never knew I wanted slip through my fingers, right when I finally realize it's been in front of me this entire time.

With this pitch, my life is on the line. The stakes are higher than anything I've ever imagined. I just hope she'll continue taking a chance on me—on us—on a possibility of a future neither of us ever let ourselves do more than dream about.

It works; she finally stops biting that lip of hers and cracks a smile.

"If last night is anything to go by, I'm pretty sure I'll be more than satisfied giving up *some* control in the bedroom. Who knew you were so talented with that wicked tongue of yours."

"I'm told I can be quite persuasive," I tease, waggling my brows playfully.

Rolling her eyes, she fills the room with laughter. "So... we're really gonna do this? Stay married?"

Before I can say anything, she gasps, "Ohmigod, what will your family think? Or Teagan for that matter? She's always teased me about having a thing for you... she's gonna give me so much shit for this..."

"I'm sure I'll get an earful from Nash, but my parents will get on board—I'm pretty sure Mom knows how I feel about you. Though she'd be too polite to say."

"Your mom knows about me?" she asks in disbelief.

"Who do you think I talked to before leaving Meyer & Cross?"

Annie lets out a loud chortle, then sighs. "Do you know I

almost didn't offer you the job because of my attraction to you?"

"What?" This is certainly news to me. "Why? That makes no sense."

"I was worried my feelings for you might've gotten in the way. But ultimately, I decided to put my feelings aside and focus on what was best for my company. And you were what was best... in more ways than one, apparently," she tacks on at the end, and I lose it with laughter.

Reaching in to tickle her, I pull her body close to mine. "Let's get one thing straight," I say when we settle down. "We're better together."

Reaching between us, she strokes my lengthening cock, and I moan in pleasure. I love that she takes what she wants, when she wants it, and isn't shy about her needs. "We are definitely much better together."

That is the end of our conversation, as lust consumes us. With her, I'm insatiable, and I don't see myself getting enough of her anytime soon. Hoping she's likely still wet from her last orgasm, I position myself above her and run my fingers through her slick folds.

Fuck, she's wet for me.

Normally, I'd stop and reach for a condom, but since our conversation last night, we decided to trust her IUD. She guides me to her entrance, and I slide into her with ease. I've never been bare with anyone. Feeling her heat against me makes my cock turn to granite, and my need for her grows. She feels incredible, and it takes everything in me not to lose myself in her instantly.

Hitching her leg over my shoulder, I deepen the angle and thrust into her the way I've quickly learned drives her wild.

As her nails scrape down my back, I moan in pleasure as I pick up the pace. When she grabs my ass, pulling me closer, I know she's close. Shifting my weight, I slide a hand between us and circle her clit, the way that makes her squirm like hell and practically speak in tongues.

"Oh, Nate. Right there. Harder. Please, Nate. I'm... So close."

Shifting slightly, I find a different angle and the way her body stills, I know it's only a matter of seconds before she explodes around me. Without a condom, I can easily feel her muscles twitch, and I lose myself in her.

Driving into her harder and harder, she grips my ass, holding me in place the minute my orgasm rips through me. My body stiffens, and pulse after pulse of pleasure shoots through me. As I drop beside her on the bed, breathless and fully sated, I can't help but wonder how each and every time gets better.

I just hope she can stay out of her head and here with me.

Chapter 4

Annie

SWIPING OPEN MY PHONE, I grin when I see Teagan calling.

We haven't talked since I left for Vegas. We have so much to catch up on, but I just want to stay in my bubble with Nate and enjoy what we've determined to be our honeymoon for the last few days.

We're due to fly home this morning. Before I left, Teagan insisted on picking me up from the airport so I can finally meet this man of hers in person. I've heard so much about Davis, and we've chatted a few times when I've been on a video call with T, but with my schedule, we haven't met in person.

"Hey, babe, how's Vegas?" Teagan asks before I can barely utter a greeting.

Oh, if only she knew. She'd probably give me the fifth degree.

Sighing from exhaustion, I grin. "Great." Though I'm not ready to come home. I'd love another week or two with just Nate before reality bites us in the ass.

"Are you still coming in at four? I can't wait to finally spend some time with you. Connor's with my mom tonight, so he'll be bummed he doesn't get to see you."

"I'll be there at four... but..." Shit, how do I say this? There's no way I can drop this news over the phone, especially since I've officially been married for nearly three days, and I haven't said boo to her.

"But what? You don't have to work, do you? I know you're busy with that new account."

"No," I rush out. "I'm not working until Monday. But would you mind if I brought... um... Nate with me? We're on the same flight."

"Nate? Holy shit... I knew something was going on with you. Of course, you can bring him. I can't wait to get to know him better. Have you had any fun in Vegas, or are you still all work and no play?"

You have no idea... but instead of spilling everything to my best friend in this instant, I deflect, the only way I can. "Oh, I've taken some time off to unwind. It's part of the reason the trip was delayed. I made a trip to Hoover Dam and even to explore the Grand Canyon."

"Wow! Good for you," she gushes. She's always on me about working so hard, so I'm certain her happiness is genuine. "Look, I gotta finish this web design, or I'll never make it to the airport."

"Sounds good. I'll see you then," I say.

THE AIRPORT IS crazy as usual when Teagan pulls up to the curb. Nate insists I hop in the front, and he'll get our bags into the car. Purse in hand, I slide in and hug Teagan. The moment Nate's door clicks shut, she zips into traffic and maneuvers her way to the airport.

There's no need for introductions. From the moment Nate started working with my company, he's met Teagan when she'd stop in to visit. Besides, with her revamping my entire website and our entire network in the last six months, he's had to call her to help troubleshoot anything that has come up.

"I'm so glad we get to do dinner and finally catch up," she says, as we get away from the airport traffic. "Davis wants you to know he's sorry he's not here himself to greet you. But he got called in this afternoon for an emergency surgery. He said he'll meet us at the house in a bit."

Turning to Nate, I quickly explain, "Davis is a pediatric orthopedic surgeon and works at Children's Hospital."

"I'm sure he's exactly where he needs to be," Nate replies.

"He's an amazing doctor. I'm sure I'm biased, but he was phenomenal with Connor when we were brought into the emergency room in Texas a few months ago. Children's Hospital is a perfect fit for him. I'm so thankful he'd already accepted the job when we met, or I have no idea where my life would be right now."

"What do you mean?" Nate asks with genuine curiosity.

"I actually met Davis when Connor visited his grandparents this summer. It's a really long story—but to be clear, we met *before* the incident. You see, when Connor broke his elbow, Davis was the doctor on call. He performed surgery, then followed up with him afterward, because he returned to

Seattle to be closer to his family. We, uh... kept in contact and officially started seeing one another rather recently."

"Wow. It's amazing how things work out, isn't it? I swear people come into your life just when they're meant to." I can hear the smile in Nate's voice without even having to look behind me. It's one I got extremely familiar with these past few days, and I can't help but wonder if that comment was meant for me, too.

"Yes, it is." Teagan nods in agreement. "Speaking of things working out, congratulations on the Worthington account. I'm so glad your hard work has paid off. Annie mentioned she actually took a break on your trip. Is this true?"

"Why would I lie about something like that?"

Teagan gives me a side-eyed glare. "Because I know you— Miss all work and no play. It must've taken an act of God or Congress to get you to *finally* relax."

Sighing heavily, I quickly huff out, "I'm not that bad."

"Yes... you are," comes from both my best friend and my husband simultaneously. Then the jerks that they are burst out laughing, knowing they're absolutely right.

Shit. He's my husband. Hell, I haven't dated anyone seriously in years, and now I'm suddenly married. How the hell do I drop a bomb like this on my best friend?

Deflect. Deflect. Deflect.

"Geesh," I grumble. "It's like you know me or something."

This earns me another laugh. But it's Nate who comes to the rescue.

"Don't worry, Teagan. I made sure she took time off and relaxed. I even convinced her to rent a car for the day, and we drove to see the Hoover Dam and the Grand Canyon. I've got pictures to prove it."

"How did you do it—get her to finally take a break?"

"Oh, I've got my ways, trust me."

Did he ever? My body heats with desire at the thought of all the things he did to me on this so-called vacation. The man can be quite persuasive, and I have no complaints at being coerced. The best part of my vacation was in the confines of our hotel room.

Teagan glances to me, and I can tell she knows something's up. I'm certain she won't call me out in front of Nate, but I'm sure the second we're alone, she'll be like a dog with a bone, grilling me for information. I was the same way when she started dating Davis, so it's only fair she gets her turn.

As we pull into Teagan's driveway, another SUV approaches and parks along the street. The way her face lights up, I know without asking, it's Davis. She quickly puts her SUV in park and gets out of the car to greet him.

Seeing her so happy and truly in love gives me hope.

They may have met months ago but officially, it's only been a few weeks. I love seeing my best friend finally find love after all these years, so I can't even tease her about her eagerness to see him. She had a rough go from the moment she knew she was pregnant. She's been a single mom ever since, never allowing herself the time to date—until Davis came and swept her off her feet.

By the time I turn to get out of the SUV, Nate's at my door, offering his hand. This simple gesture has my heart skipping a beat. He's always been thoughtful, but with a squeeze of my hand, he makes me wish I'd skipped on dinner tonight. I'm truly not ready for our bubble to burst with reality.

When his hand glides to the base of my back as we walk toward Davis, a sense of both excitement and peace wash over me. My body craves more of him, and yet I feel grounded and at home at the same time.

Before I can give it too much thought, I quickly rush to greet Teagan's new man.

"Hey, Davis, it's great to finally see you in person," I say, leaning in for a hug. For a second, I'm sure I've caught him off guard, but he quickly recovers. There's no way I can't hug the man who makes my best friend so happy.

"Same, Annie. Teagan's been dying to get us together."

Teagan shrugs. "What can I say, I want my favorite people together... sue me."

Shaking my head, I can't help but laugh at her antics.

"Davis, I'd like you to meet Nate, my..." Shit. What do I introduce him as?

Before I can come up with a response, Nate steps up and shakes Davis's hand and supplies the answer, "Husband. I'm Annie's husband."

To me, he turns with a shit-eating grin. "God. That's the first time I've introduced myself with that title. It certainly has a nice ring to it, don't ya think?"

"What?" Teagan shrieks, and I swear the dogs six blocks over are suddenly on high alert.

Well, shit... I guess the cat's out of the bag.

Shrugging, I hold up my hand, ring finger on display, and I

swear Teagan gasps so hard, she sucks all the air from our vicinity.

"You. Got. Married?" Teagan sputters, then her voice raises. "And you're just telling me this now?"

I can see her wheels spinning out of control, then she rushes to squeeze the ever-living life right out of me. "Ohmigod! You're married!" We rock side to side for a moment before she gasps and pulls back to look from me to Nate.

"Wait... just how the hell did this happen? You wouldn't even admit you liked him, let alone that you were seeing him... have you been holding out on me this entire time?"

I vaguely hear Davis say, "Congratulations, man." But I'm too focused on Teagan that I have no idea what's said between Davis and Nate.

I'd never lie to her, and I need to set the record straight.

"No, I haven't been holding out on you—well, maybe for the past few days but trust me—this is an entirely new development."

She opens her mouth to say something, then quickly clamps it shut. She slowly looks from me to Nate, then returns her attention to me as she shakes her head in confusion.

"Look," Davis says, getting both of our attention. "Let's go inside. I'll open a bottle of wine, and the two of you can talk more while Nate and I start the grill and get dinner settled." Turning his attention to Nate, he asks, "That okay with you?"

"Sure. Just tell me what needs to be done."

The moment the guys step out back, and we're alone, wine in hand, Teagan raises a brow in my direction and demands,

"Spill it. How on earth did you go from barely admitting you had a crush on that man outside—to being his *wife*?"

"I... uh... Shit. It's complicated." I finally admit when I realize I'm not sure where to begin.

"Uncomplicate it, Annabelle. You're the most planned-out, predictable person I know. You work hard and won't even let yourself consider dating anyone because you're so focused on building your company. Though now I'm fairly certain that man out there has everything to do with you not dating recently. But hell, you wouldn't even admit to me that you've liked him, and I'm your supposed best friend."

When I start to protest, she cuts me off, "Oh, get that look off your face. This is me you're talking to. I'm not mad; I'm just trying to understand *how* this happened. Have you been seeing each other or has something been going on during all those late hours you've been working together?"

"First, nothing happened until Vegas—though you and I both know I've been falling for him, despite the fact that I've been fighting like hell to resist it. I mean he's my employee for crying out loud. True, in recent months, he's become a close friend, but this isn't exactly something I planned. But for once... hell, I just went with it."

"What do you mean—you went with it?"

Taking a deep breath, I ponder my words to explain it best. But this is Teagan, and we don't hold back—we never have.

"Okay... nothing happened until after we pitched the Worthington account, I swear. Nate saw I was getting in my head and insisted we go out to celebrate, leaving it all in the boardroom. He made me promise I'd stop overthinking and just live in the moment."

I can hear the awe in her voice when she whispers, "Wow, he really does know you, doesn't he?"

"Yeah, I think he does," I admit on a sigh. "Anyway—long story short. He insisted we go to dinner and hit up a club his brother hooked him up with. We were drinking, we were dancing, and it felt amazing to be in his arms. Eventually, we walked the strip and stopped to watch the fountain. It was there we kissed for the first time."

"You'd never kissed before Vegas?" she asks in disbelief.

"Nope. I'm telling you—*nothing* happened before this trip. I swear."

"But how'd you go from zero to married? I mean. That's a huge leap—especially for you, Ann."

"Yeah. Tell me about it," I mutter, rolling my eyes, then I laugh as I admit, "That's the question of the century. One minute, I was kissing the hell out of him; the next, I started to get in my head. Which he stopped in an instant, by the way."

"Really?"

"Yep. I started worrying about working together and what would happen when things end—because let's face it, they always do. But then he shocked the shit out of me and countered with, *what if they don't.*"

Teagan's hand flies to her face as she gasps, "Ohmigod."

Ignoring her, I continue, "Apparently, I'm not the only one who's been harboring feelings. He got down on one knee right then and there and proposed to prove he has zero intentions of going anywhere."

Teagan's eyes nearly bug out when she asks, "What the hell? How does declaring your feelings zip you into the fast lane for marriage? What kind of logic is that?"

Shrugging, I slowly admit, "Drunk logic?" Because yeah... I got nothing.

"Just how much had you been drinking?"

"Enough to think his logic made sense, but not so much that I didn't know what I was doing," I quietly admit.

Now that I'm saying it aloud, it's the craziest logic I've ever heard. *I mean, who gets married to prove they're in it for the long haul?*

I do, apparently.

Teagan chews on her lower lip, as I can see her wheels spinning. Eventually, she asks, "How do you feel about this logic now?"

Taking in a deep breath so I can process her words, I deeply exhale before responding with my heart, "Honestly, this may be the most spontaneous thing I've ever done, but I can't say I regret anything. Being with Nate is nothing like I've ever experienced."

She studies me carefully, the way only a best friend can, before quietly asking, "So you love him?"

Again, I take a moment to think about my words before I respond, "I haven't actually said the words, but if I'm being honest, I think I've been falling for him for a while now. Little by little, he's wormed his way into my heart, and I'd rather take this chance to be with him, than worry about the risks at this point. This will sound crazy, but I think with Nate, it has to be all or nothing."

"Well, you certainly went all in," she teases.

"That I did," I admit on a laugh, taking another sip of my wine.

She suddenly gasps, then laughs as she demands, "Tell me you didn't get hitched by Elvis or through a drive-thru chapel or anything as cliché as Vegas is known for."

"For your information, we were married in the chapel at our hotel. As we walked by a dress shop, Nate insisted on doing some things right. He insisted I pick out a dress, while he ran a quick errand of his own."

Teagan's eyes widen as she asks, "What could he possibly run off to do?"

"He didn't want a simple band that the chapel could provide."

"No shit. Talk about go big or go home. At least Nate's got some seriously good taste. That ring is gorgeous."

Looking down, I get butterflies recalling the first time I laid eyes on it. "I had no idea he'd picked one up. When the officiant asked if we had rings, I nearly fainted when I saw the blue Tiffany box come out of his pocket. He even picked up a matching band for himself. I hadn't even thought of it."

"Uh, just how much time did you have between the proposal and the ceremony?"

Wrinkling my nose, I try to remember. "An hour. Maybe? I don't know. It was kinda a blur."

"No shit, Sherlock," she chortles. "Yours has to be one of the shortest engagements in history! Did you at least get any pictures?"

Frantically pulling my phone out of my pocket, I swipe it

open, scroll to the shared file from the chapel, and send it to Teagan's phone. "There. Now you're officially the first person I've sent wedding photos to."

Teagan swipes open her phone and gasps. When she looks up, tears are in her eyes. "Oh, Annabelle. You look incredible. That dress was perfect for you."

I'd chosen a vintage style, ruffle hem dress. It had a round neckline, and a high waist to accentuate my curves in just the right way. The three-quarter sleeves and flair of the skirt reminded me of something Katherine Hepburn would've worn.

"Thanks. The moment I saw it, I knew that was the dress. There was only one left—and it was my size. I just knew it was the one."

"You looked stunning, and Nate looked amazing, too, in his navy suit."

"He looked sexier than ever while waiting for me at the end of the aisle. If you keep clicking through the file, we got the entire ceremony recorded."

Instead of frantically flipping through the images to find the video, Teagan puts her phone down and reaches for my hand.

"I've known you forever, Annie. That look on your face, in that picture, is one of a woman in love."

"You don't think I've made a terrible mistake?" I ask, admitting my deepest fear.

Slowly, she shakes her head. "Does he make you happy?"

"He's always made me happy," I whisper.

"Well, If you're happy, I'm happy for you." Standing, she

reaches for my hand and pulls me into a hug. "I love you, Annie, and I'm certain things will work out the way they are meant to be."

When she lets go, she tilts her head to the backyard. "What do you say we get our guys so they can feel safe to join us. I'm dying to know more details about that sexy man of yours, but I think we've left them to their own devices long enough. Let's see what kind of trouble they're getting up to."

Chapter 5

Nate

OVERALL, I'd say dinner with Annie's friends was a success. Since all of us celebrated with drinks throughout the evening, Annie ordered us a ride. When we arrive at her place, I unload our bags from the trunk, and the car quickly drives away.

Suddenly, she turns to me and gasps, catching me completely off guard.

"Ohmigod. I didn't even think about asking if you wanted to go to your place. I swear, I must've been on autopilot because I'm dying to sleep in my own bed after being away for the last few days."

Leaning in, I kiss the worry off her lips. "I want to be where you are. After traveling all day, I'm ready to haul you off to bed and have my way with you again."

This elicits a beautiful laugh. "You and your one-track mind. We need to talk about some things, Nate."

As she unlocks her door, I set the luggage down on the porch beside her and stop her from entering. "Look, Annie. I know we need to talk, but we've got the rest of our lives to figure out the details. For now, can we just keep living in the moment?"

"For now," she sighs. "But we do need to talk at some point."

She slowly nibbles on her lower lip, which is her tell for when she's overthinking things. This just won't do. "You promised to stay with me—Annabelle Bellinger, in the here and now."

Before she can respond, I lean down, swooping her off her feet, and lift her into my arms with ease. Carrying her through the threshold, I can't help but laugh at her flabbergasted expression.

Her laughter echoes off the walls as she swats at me. "What are you doing? Put me down."

"We may have gone about this differently from most, but I'm not about to deprive you of everything that comes with getting married."

Slowly, I set her down, letting her body slide against mine until her feet hit the floor.

"Nate..." she draws out as her arms loop around my neck. "You seem to think of everything."

"Hardly." I laugh as I lean my lips closer to hers. "I'm just making shit up as I go."

"You don't have me fooled, Nate Bellinger. You're a total romantic at heart."

Clutching my heart, I feign being wounded. "You say that like it's a bad thing."

"No... I... I've never seen this side of you, and it's... well... I wasn't expecting it."

"Did you expect me to be a selfish ass?"

Vehemently, she shakes her head. "No. I've never let myself go there with you, so I have no idea what I thought."

Suddenly, her expression turns pensive, and I can see the moment her wheels spin again.

I know we need to talk, but I'm not ready for our bubble of bliss to burst. Needing more of her, I lower my head, pressing my lips to hers. It's not nearly enough, but it gets my point across—she needs to stay in this moment with me. I've witnessed her plenty over the last few years obsessing over the littlest of details.

When we pull apart, I raise a brow and challenge, "Well, I think it's high time you start thinking that way. If..."

Shit—I don't want to sound like I'm not into this.

I may not have acted on my feelings until Vegas, but it doesn't mean they weren't there. Hell, I never expected we'd get married after literally only our first kiss, but it doesn't mean I'm any less committed to her. My drunken proposal just took things to a new level. At the time, it was the only way that made sense for us to be together, and days later, I still have zero regrets... especially now that I've tasted her luscious lips, slipped inside her, and made her scream my name like I've only ever dreamed of.

I may get lost in my head for a minute, but I quickly continue with, "I mean... *when* we're together, you need to know you're a priority. I want to get to know you—the side of you you've worked hard to keep hidden since we've met. I want to see you get decked out in one of your sexy-as-sin dresses and go out on the town, I want to have casual evenings, and I want everything in between. I'm sure there's gonna be times I totally fuck up—and I fully expect you to call me on it. But my point is, if we're gonna give this a go, we need to give it a chance. That means I'm going to do all the things—so you may as well get used to it."

Reaching for my shirt, she pulls me close. "I think that's quite possibly the most romantic thing anyone's ever said to me. I've always known you're a take-charge type of guy, but witnessing you throw down the gauntlet like that has me feeling hot and bothered."

"Well, we can't have that now," I tease as she reaches for the fly of my jeans.

"We *will* talk about things, but first, I think I should give you a tour of my place..."

I could give two shits about her house.

She fists my jeans harder and tugs me down the hall.

Hell, I've never had a woman take charge like this, and I like it.

Having no choice but to follow, she points out rooms as we go. "Living room... kitchen... bathroom..." When we walk past the stairs, she quickly mumbles, "Home office and spare bedrooms are upstairs."

When we reach the end of the hall, she opens the door, and I couldn't tell you anything about her bedroom beyond the fact that she has a large bed on the opposite wall.

The moment we're close to the bed, she turns and faces me. Her eyes heat as her grip on my waistband tightens. Then before I can take in my next breath, her hands release their hold on my fly and slide around the band to my ass. The way she licks her lips as her hands dip into my boxers to squeeze my ass makes my dick stiffen and ready for action.

Annie's always had an effect on me, but knowing she's no longer out of reach or off limits makes me want to cash in every single fantasy I've had about her over the years. Forcing myself to remain still and allowing her to stay in control is harder than I would've thought.

Shit, now's not the time to be making puns. It only makes me harder.

Just when I don't think I can stand here much longer without taking control, her hands slide down my hips and drop down my thighs, taking both my boxers and my jeans with her. Annie proved her adventurous side in our short time together in Vegas, but I'm still not prepared for when her body drops to her knees right along with my jeans.

"These need to go," she demands as my pants reach my ankles.

Quickly, I toe off my shoes and step out of my jeans, kicking them to the side.

Annabelle Holstings on her knees before me is a sight to behold. When she reaches for my bobbing cock, giving it a light squeeze, I nearly lose my mind. I'm mesmerized by the way she peers through thick lashes to meet my gaze. Her blue eyes heat with desire as her tongue sweeps under the head of my cock and swirls around the tip.

"Fuck, Annie..." comes out on a groan as I force my hands to remain frozen at my sides. I want nothing more than to dig a hand into her thick golden-brown hair at the base of her neck and fuck her beautiful mouth.

Even with my cock filling her mouth, I can feel more than see her triumphant smile, as her lips tighten around me. When she fists the base of my shaft and takes me in further, I have to break eye contact because I will completely lose myself if I keep watching.

Tilting my head to the sky, I close my eyes, feeling every sensation, each swipe of her glorious tongue. In and out, swirling around the tip, before gripping my cock tighter and nearly swallowing me again. Over and over, she repeats this pattern, until I feel my knees go weak.

It feels so fucking incredible. Needing to touch her, I allow my hands to slide into her hair, but my grip on the base of her neck remains loose, letting her control the pace. When she hollows her cheeks and sucks harder as she retreats, the base of my spine tingles with the impending signs of an orgasm brewing.

As if I'm not teetering on the brink of an epic explosion, the vixen uses the exact moment my balls creep into my body to cup them with her free hand. As I fight to stay under control of my body and make this moment last, she somehow squeezes my sac with her palm as she massages that spot right behind them with her fingers.

"Fuck me," I growl as she sucks me even harder.

"Shit, Annie. I'm close," comes out frantic, as I'm doing everything in my power to hold off long enough for her to release me.

Tapping her shoulder in warning, I beg, "Seriously, babe..." I pant. "I'm gonna come."

But she reacts as if I've just thrown down a challenge, rather than a warning. The glorious woman kneeling before me doubles down on her efforts, sucking me entirely into her mouth. Her tongue flattens and drags along my shaft with each and every thrust of her mouth, until I'm fairly certain nothing I say is coherent.

I have no idea what comes out of my mouth, as I grab onto her for dear life, so I won't pass out from the pleasure.

Annie's hand slides along my balls, squeezing and massaging me as she hollows her cheeks and tips me over the edge. Pulse after pulse, my cum slides down her throat as she milks the most explosive orgasm of my life out of me. My legs lose all sense of feeling and if I wasn't gripping her shoulder like a vise, I'd swear my legs would drop out from under me.

She licks up every last drop until I reach the point where over-sensitivity kicks in, and I practically beg her to stop.

Slowly, she releases my cock, leaving it to bob at will, while the last twitches of my incredible orgasm subside. Reaching under her shoulders, I pull her up to stand before me.

For a moment, we just stare wordlessly at one another while I brush some wayward strands of her long hair behind her ear. Running the pad of my thumb over her swollen lips, I whisper, "That. Was. Incredible. How is it that each time with you it gets even better?"

I don't expect an answer, but a wide grin forms as she admits, "I don't know."

Slanting my mouth over hers, I feel her exhale heavily. Not

giving her a chance to say another word, my lips crash onto hers. She tastes of me. She tastes of her. She tastes of us as I devour her completely.

My hands roam her body, and it's then I realize she's still dressed, and I never got my shirt off. This needs to be rectified. Without letting my lips leave her body, I kiss down her neck while my hand works at untucking her shirt and unbuttoning her jeans.

Breaking our kiss, I pant, "You are entirely overdressed for this occasion."

Laughing, she looks me over from head to toe. "The whole socks and open shirt thing you've got going on, may just be my favorite look for you."

Shaking my head, I roll my eyes. Shrugging out of my shirt, I scoff. "Don't be ridiculous."

I feel each and every inch of her eyes as they roam over my body. Slowly, she removes her own shirt, then runs her tongue over her lower lip. "You're right. That's a much better look on you."

Even though I've seen her naked plenty of times over these past few days, she still renders me speechless. My mouth dries as she slowly slides her jeans down her body. It's as if she's giving me my own private strip tease, and my heart thuds out of my chest at the thought of seeing more of her.

By the time she's completely naked, my patience and self-control have disappeared. Immediately, I close the distance between us, reaching for the base of her neck to angle her face to meet mine. Before my lips meet hers, I growl, "I need to taste every inch of you."

Needing time to recover, I focus my efforts on her.

My lips crash onto hers, and our bodies intertwine as we devour one another as if we haven't just spent the last few days exploring one another. I love learning what makes Annie tick. With our tongues dancing together as we nip and suck, we find the rhythm we've perfected. Her skin feels silky smooth as my hands roam from her back to her thighs. At the same time, her arms wrap around my neck, fingers play in my hair, and her erect nipples press against my chest, as if she needs me closer.

Wanting her splayed out on the bed, I grip her upper thighs with ease, lifting her higher on my body. As if we've done this a million times, her legs wrap around my waist, and she clings to me as I crawl up the end of the bed, until we're both in the center.

"God, you're so impatient." She laughs. "I could've helped."

"But my way was more efficient. See," I say, leaning back on my thighs with a victorious grin. "God, you're beautiful, all sprawled out naked before me. This is definitely something I would've missed if we'd stayed standing. Now I can watch you squirming like hell before making you come."

"Gosh... you let a guy give you a few orgasms, and he suddenly thinks he knows all about you..."

"This is more than orgasms... and you know it," I counter with a smirk, knowing full well she's throwing down a challenge of her own.

She's competitive as hell and isn't afraid to share her sexual desires. She also knows I don't back down from a challenge either. I fucking love pleasuring her and won't stop until she's satisfied.

Her body comes alive when she's turned on. It's hot as hell to watch how responsive she is. I can play her body like it was made for only me. Every sigh, gasp, or moan leads us both to the most pleasure—and that's something I'll never tire of.

She may think she's sassy and in control, but I've got news for her. I've been paying attention for years to her cues. They may not have been sexual, but I've learned to read her pretty well. I see the things she doesn't say aloud, and I consider myself a quick study.

Leaning forward, I brace my hands on each side of her shoulders and stare into her eyes. I can feel her heat as I hover above her, keeping my weight from crushing her. For a long moment, I just stare into her eyes, our breathing getting more sporadic, and we haven't even done anything.

"For the record," I whisper hoarsely, "I'm all about *you*, not the orgasms. Though those are a fantastic bonus, I'm not gonna lie. But seriously, Annie, I'm here for the good, the bad, the ugly, *and* the toe-curling, mind-blowing, body-wracking, coma-inducing Os. A guy's gotta have standards, ya know?"

Rolling her eyes as her finger traces my cheek, she mumbles, "Promises... promises."

My mouth crashes onto hers, and words are forgotten as I show her exactly what I mean. Slowly kissing down her body, I enjoy every moment from her jawline, across her collarbone, to her beautifully pert nipples. Her hips gyrate against me in slow circles, and that's all I need to know I'm on the right track.

Nudging her legs open wider, I readjust my body to gain access to her most delicate flesh.

My mouth pays homage to her breasts while my fingers roam against her ribs, down her outer legs, and along the valley of her inner thighs, repeating the pattern until she's breathless and moaning. My fingers tease and circle every place of her soft and sensitive flesh, but where I know she wants me most, and her hips move faster.

By accident, I find when I massage her, the outside of her lower lips and along her hood, it's almost as much as a turn-on for her as when I play with her clit. She practically bounces off the bed when I finally flick her clit and pull her nipple into my mouth, teasing it with my tongue. "Fuck, Nate..." she practically screams, and I know I've hit my mark.

"Do that again. Yes. Right there. Keep playing with me like that."

Changing the angle of my hand, I'm able to do as she's asked, and her body is even more responsive. She pants, moans, and rocks her hips into my hand. After a few more strokes, I add another layer. Slipping my middle finger into her tight channel, I feel her inner walls grip around me.

"God... I need you, Nate..."

"You've got me," I quickly assure her. "I'm right here."

Shaking her head, she disagrees, "No. I want you... in me... now. I need to come on your cock, not on your fingers or tongue. I wanna feel full... and explode... with you."

My dick hears her suggestion loud and clear and bobs to attention against her thigh. "I can wait, babe," I remind her.

"This is about you," I say, sucking her other nipple into my mouth.

"I can't," she pants. "I need you to fuck me hard... and fast," she begs. "I'm so close..."

I don't need to be told twice. In a split second, I'm repositioned on the bed and lined up with her entrance. I know without a doubt, she's wet and ready for me, but I don't want to hurt her, so I slowly ease my way in, giving her time to adjust.

"Nate," she growls, gripping my ass and pulling me closer as she thrusts her hips into me. "Fuck me... hard."

Sliding in, I bottom out, only to quickly retreat and do it again. Fuck. She feels amazing. Her heat grips me and pulls me in as I thrust in deep and repeat the process. Her body clings to me as our hips piston together in the most incredible rhythm.

After a while, I need to be deeper inside her. When I pull out completely, she moans in frustration. But the minute I tap her thigh and flip her to her stomach, she moans, "Yes..."

Bracing herself on all fours, she presents her glorious ass to me. Her pussy is slick with desire and waiting for me.

Taking a moment to appreciate the goddess before me I moan, "God, you're beautiful," before running a finger through her slick folds.

"Stop teasing me, Nate..." she groans as I pinch her clit the way she enjoys.

"Always trying to top from the bottom," I muse.

Before she can respond, I spread her knees wider and slide into her from behind. My throbbing cock hits her at a different angle and the sound she elicits into the room lets me know I'm on the right track. It doesn't take long before we've found our rhythm.

The room fills with the sounds of us. Moans, pants, slapping of skin, and squeaks from the bed. As I get lost in all that's her, she continues getting tighter and tighter around me.

"So close... Right... there... harder..."

The second I reach around her body to stroke her clit, her body tightens, and I know it's only a matter of seconds before she's tumbling over the edge. Needing to be there with her, I thrust harder, racing her to the finish line.

My spine tingles and energy explodes as the pulsing of her pussy begins.

Thrusting hard once, twice, three more times, I release into her.

"Fuck..." I growl as there's a motion I don't expect mid orgasm.

We're suddenly falling forward, and the bed is no longer parallel with the floor.

On instinct, I brace myself against the wall as we fall, so I don't crush her. Of course, in the process, I slide out of her, and my cum shoots everywhere.

She lands with an "umph" on the mattress when it settles on the floor.

As I take a moment to process this new predicament, I quickly spit out, "Are you okay?"

She's shaking and for a second, I think she might be hurt, so I scramble off the bed, wet dick and all, and turn her over to see where she might be hurt.

But the brat's not hurt. She has tears running down her face, but she's laughing uncontrollably. "Ohmigod," she gasps. "We... broke the bed."

"You told me you wanted it harder." I shrug, awkwardly pulling her to a standing position. "You sure you're okay?" I say through a laugh.

"I'm good... but I hope you're okay with pulling the mattress to the floor because I'm not sleeping in my great-grandma's bed with you in the other room. That's a family heirloom, and I'm not about to break that, too."

Looking at the dilapidated bed, the entire headboard literally broke from the frame as the wood is splintered on each side of the rail. The mattress leans toward the wall, and I'm not sure there's enough glue in the world to make it sturdy again.

"Yeah, I'm thinking this is beyond repair," I admit before turning to her and brushing her hair from her face. "Seriously, are you okay?"

Her skin is flush, her hair has that just been thoroughly fucked look, sticking up in all directions, but she couldn't look more beautiful.

Reaching around to touch her back, she cringes. "I... uh... need a shower. Wanna join me, then we can clean this up and actually get some sleep."

I love how she takes everything in stride.

"Sorry about that." I cringe, looking from her to the bed.

Her beautiful laugh fills the room. "Why? I'm not. That was hot. Besides, how often can you say we broke a bed? Wait... if this is a habit for you, I'm not sure I need to know."

"Oh my God, woman. You know how to inflate my ego." I

chuckle at her sudden backtracking. She's adorable when her unnecessary jealous side shows.

Just what kind of life does she think I lived before her?

"But for the record. No, that was definitely a first." Waggling my brows, I reach for her. "Though I'm happy to help you break more, if that's your new standard for amazing sex."

Shaking her head, she turns and walks toward a room I can only presume is the bathroom. "If you think your ego can fit in the shower with me, you're welcome to join."

Chapter 6

Annie

AS I'M SITTING at my desk, drinking copious amounts of coffee, my mind keeps replaying the events of these last few days. I know Nate and I have a million things we need to talk about, but I won't deny I haven't enjoyed each and every moment with him.

I still can't believe we broke my bed. He quickly showered with me, then left to get ready while he dismantled what was left of the frame and got the mattress settled on the floor. I can only imagine what the neighbors will think when he put it out by the curb this morning before we left for work.

Nate had an early meeting with a client, so he ordered a car to take him to his place to grab his car and change into some clean clothes. This left me time to get ready at a leisurely pace and get into the office.

Being out of town for nearly a week, I've got plenty to catch up on. Not only do we need to nail down the details of the Worthington account, but we have other clients who have projects they need completed in the coming weeks.

Thankfully, Trina, my personal assistant, keeps us organized and on top of the projects we've committed to, or I'd be on a sinking ship. My head is in the clouds, and I can't stop thinking about Nate. I still can't believe how much my life has changed in a matter of a week. Not only am I involved with someone, but I'm married. I certainly didn't have that on my bingo card for this year—or this lifetime for that matter.

Nate Bellinger certainly has swept me off my feet. He's made me realize I've been missing out on a lot since starting this company. Not only have I had more earth-shattering Os in the last five days than the last five years, but he's made me realize there's more to life than working twenty-four-seven.

Now that we've landed this big account, I can finally hire the people I need to help me with all the details necessary to grow our client base. Holstings' Creative has been at capacity with just Nate, Trina, and me. I've made it work by putting in the hours and working nearly six to seven days a week. But I can't keep that schedule forever and frankly, after one week with Nate, I realize I don't want to.

I need to find what others mean when they have a work-life balance.

I want my company to succeed, don't get me wrong, but in one short week, Nate's made me realize I want more than just financial success for my future. But can Nate and I navigate these suddenly murky waters we've created for ourselves?

The buzzer on my phone knocks me out of my thoughts, as Trina's voice comes through. "I know you said you didn't want to be disturbed, but Nate's asking to see you. Can I send him in?"

A smile spreads across my lips, and my belly flips at just the thought of him being right outside the door. "Sure, Trina. Send him in."

Standing, I walk around my desk to greet him.

He's changed into a navy button-down shirt and a pair of gray trousers. We're pretty casual here in the office when we're not meeting with clients, but this color on him has always been among my favorites.

The minute the door clicks behind him, his grin melts my panties. It's heated and full of need as he closes the distance and says, "I didn't think it was possible to miss you so much."

Reaching out, he pulls me to him as I admit, "Me, too. I've been trying to focus all morning and doing a shit job of it."

Leaning in, his lips brush against mine, and he kisses me all too quickly before pulling back with a grin.

Reaching for my hand, he squeezes as he says, "Well, that makes two of us. Thank God, Jim Matthews is so full of himself to notice. I'll get what he wants done later this week and get it back to him by next week."

"Would you have time to sit in on some interviews? Now that we have the Worthington account, I'd like to do a final interview to bring in some help around here. I've got it narrowed down to four applicants, but we'll only be able to hire two, for now."

"You're the boss," he reminds me. "I'm sure you'll pick the best ones."

"Well," I sigh, trying to figure out how to broach the subject without making things weird between us. "We've talked about you taking a bigger role in the company—before going to Vegas, and I know you've casually mentioned buying into the company as a partner. Is this something you're still interested in?"

Nate's quiet for a long moment, and then he says, "Let's sit down and discuss this further."

Unsure of what to expect, I do as he says, sitting in one of my guest chairs as he does the other. Thankfully, I don't have to wait long for him to share his thoughts.

His eyes never leave mine as he takes in a long breath and slowly exhales. "We've always been straight with one another. I meant what I said in Vegas. My priority is being with you. No offense but fuck the company—if us being together makes you leery in any way."

What the fuck does that mean?

Shaking his head, he cuts me off before I can respond, "No, you don't get it. I value our relationship more than I do being your partner in the business and if you think that will get in our way, I can find another source of employment."

"Uh... that wouldn't help anything. I hear your point, loud and clear. But walking away isn't an option. Professionally," I feel the need to clarify, "this company wouldn't be the same without you. We've spent the better part of two years building this to get it to where it is."

"But you've put up the capital and start-up money to get Holstings' Creative afloat. We'll have to look at the numbers specifically, but I'm fairly certain you're no longer funneling personal funds to keep it going, are you?"

"No. I haven't had to since that first year," I proudly admit. It was hell at first, and my house is mortgaged to the hilt, but it's definitely running in the black, and I'm starting to repay myself for the start-up costs.

"I'll tell you what. Why don't you have the accountant run

the numbers and the lawyers draw up a partnership agreement? Before the whole business of us getting married, we'd discussed you keeping a bigger claim on the company. So, I say we stick to the sixty-forty agreement we've talked about. After all, it's your name on the door. We've made a reputation as Holstings', so I'd rather keep it—if that's okay with you."

Then he winks, and I can't help but laugh when he tacks on, "Even if neither of us officially have that as our last name—it's what the company is known as."

Crossing my arms, I lean back in my chair. "Is that your way of asking me if I'm taking your last name?"

Shrugging, he asks, "Is that even something you'd consider? I mean. I'd never assume anything. But I won't lie when I say it's crossed my mind."

Hell, it hasn't crossed my mind once. Some wife I am.

Before I can say anything, he reaches out and pats my leg. "Look, Annabelle. Nothing has to be decided today. I personally don't care what your last name is, as long as you're mine."

"Caveman much?" I tease, though the thought of being called his sends tingles up my spine and warmth throughout my body. I love that he knows what he wants, and I'm apparently it.

Rolling his eyes, he sighs as he leans toward me, so that we're almost touching but not quite. "You know what I mean. As long as we're together, I'm not such a Neanderthal that I can't respect your independence. You've worked hard both personally and professionally to get to where you are, and I'm proud of you for it. I have no idea what it would be like to change my identity—just because I'm married—so I won't ask that of you. But the thought of being Mr. and Mrs. Bellinger does have a nice ring to it—especially if we get to the point where we consider having kids."

"Whoa, whoa, whoa. Slow your roll, Bellinger. We literally kissed for the first time—*last week*. We've gone from that to married, in a matter of two point nine seconds, and *now you're talking kids?*" Even I can hear my voice rise in disbelief at the end. I mean, the man certainly doesn't hold back.

It's not that I'm actually panicked, but I have to give him a hard time.

"Okay... I've thought about having kids—someday—in the future, with a fictitious husband and whatnot. But I've barely given myself the chance to date in recent years, so this isn't a conversation I'm prepared for."

"Okay." He chuckles. "Roll is slowed." Then he's quiet for a moment before jumping to his feet excitedly. "Let's start with a date. I've got a two o'clock meeting in Tacoma with my brother. What do you say I pick you up at seven, and we'll officially have our first date?"

"What was dinner and the club in Vegas?"

His eyes shine with delight as his beautiful lips spread into a grin. "That was getting you out of your head. Tonight, you're going to go home and change into a sexy dress that will render me speechless. Don't put too much thought into it; any dress will do—as it happens on the daily with you."

"Now you're just being silly."

"Pack an overnight bag because I think we should test out my bed. You know, to make sure it can handle us. Besides, I have a king-size, and I live closer, so the commute won't be as long tomorrow."

This is news to me, as I have no idea where he lives.

But the thought of trying to break another bed does make my imagination run wild.

Glancing at his watch, he returns his gaze to mine. "What do you say, Annie? Do we have a date?"

"Uh... sure," I mutter, "though you seem to think I'm a sure thing."

Taking my hand, he pulls me to stand before him. Leaning down, he brushes his lips to mine before pulling back and looking me in the eye.

"For the record, it's not about the sex, Annabelle. I don't care if we ever have sex again—though that would be a shame because let's face it, we're fire in the sheets, and it would be a tragedy to never experience it again. But seriously, I just wanna spend time with you and wake up with you in my arms."

If he wasn't holding me right now, I'm fairly certain I'd melt into a pile on the floor. Nate Bellinger just totally swooped me off my feet, and my heart is beyond full.

I can't even think.

Thankfully, I don't have to because he presses his lips to mine, and I get lost in all that's Nate. Damn, this man can kiss. It's all-consuming and makes me feel more cherished than I've ever imagined. If I didn't know better, it also makes me feel—loved.

But of course, it's too soon for anything like that.

Chapter 7

Nate

I LOVE SEEING MY BROTHER, but man, do I hate the traffic getting to Tacoma. Even midday, the journey from Seattle to his place is unpredictable. I swear, the minute you pass the Tacoma Dome, the city wants you to stroll past it at a snail's pace, so you can enjoy the beauty along with the water from Puget Sound behind it.

Today, Nash and I are meeting to discuss the marketing for the business he founded in college. With this season being in full swing, he doesn't have time to travel to me—thus my reason for the commute. Not only do I design and market his personal merchandise, but I'm also in charge of marketing for his foundation.

Even though he's a professional kicker for the NFL, he still finds the time to run summer camps and clinics for soccer. Originally, it was a way to make some cash on the side as soccer was his life—until he fell into football accidentally. But that's a story for a different day. When he eventually went pro, he turned his soccer enterprise into a foundation—but still needed someone to market and promote it, and that's where I come in.

When I finally get to his exit, I'm relieved to move past

the traffic that's basically parked on the freeway. Sometimes, this commute takes less than thirty minutes, but today, it took over an hour. Thankfully, it's only a little past two when I arrive.

"Hey, man, how's it going?" Nash says as he pulls me in for a man hug, and he slaps my back in greeting at the door. It's been over a month since we've seen one another, and I've certainly missed him.

"It's good. Thanks again for getting me tickets to that club last week. I owe you—big time."

Walking into his kitchen, he opens the fridge. "Can I get you anything to drink?"

"Water is good," I say, sitting on a bar stool at the kitchen island. He's already got his work sitting here, so I might as well take a seat.

"I've only gone one time, but that club was worth the hype. Hey, you never said, who did you end up using the extra ticket on? Don't tell me, you actually let your hair down and hooked up with some rando in Vegas."

God, if he only knew.

"No. *For your information,*" I emphasize to get my point across, "I didn't *hook up* with a random girl."

His shit-eating grin spreads from ear to ear. "But you did hook up... with someone."

Running a hand down my face, I look to the ceiling for how to explain this properly.

"Holy shit!" Nash gasps and points at me. "What the hell is *that* on your finger?"

Fuck, this is not how I planned on telling him.

I always shoot straight with him—today shouldn't be any different. So, I state the obvious.

"It's a ring."

"No shit, Sherlock. I can see for myself it's a ring. Who the hell did you hook up with in Vegas?"

"It's not a hook-up," I chastise. There's no way I want him to think anything less of Annie.

I can tell the second Nash puts it together because his eyes bug out, and his mouth drops to the floor. If he wasn't leaning against the counter behind him, I'd swear his ass would hit the floor, too. "Holy shit. You're married."

"Uh... that would be correct."

"If it's not a random chick—then are you telling me you finally put the moves on Annabelle Holstings?"

"I didn't just put the moves on her," I point out, looking at the ring on my finger. "I married her."

"What the actual fuck, man? Are you kidding me?"

"Do I look like I'm kidding?" I counter and swear his eyes look as if they're about to pop out of their sockets. I swear, it's not healthy. There's so much white showing, and I'm getting a little concerned.

"Okay. Back up. Explain. I thought she was just your boss. You swore up and down nothing was going on with the two of you. I mean you swore on Nana's grave, so are you telling me you were lying?"

"There wasn't. I'd never even kissed her until that night after the club."

"And yet, you're married less than a week later. How does that happen?"

"With the magic of the fountain, a touch of alcohol, and a lot of hormones?" I spit out, though the end comes out as a question, even to my ears. So, I quickly tack on, "I also had a lot of negotiating. I... uh... somehow managed to convince her to take a chance on me—as more than her employee. When she questioned my logic and worried things could end terribly, I wanted to prove I was in this for the long haul. You know as well as I do, she's the one I've spent the last year comparing all others to. So... I... uh... dropped to one knee and proposed. I mean, go big or go home, right?"

My brother is silent for a full minute—maybe longer.

Nash is never silent. He's always got something to say and if I wasn't so nervous for his reaction, I'd almost find this comical. He's my best friend in the entire world, and his opinion means a lot.

I'm certain he thinks I've lost all my marbles, but honestly, when it comes to Annie, I don't care what others think. After spending these last few days together, and finally grasping what I've been missing, I don't want it any other way.

"So... you love her." His words come out as a statement, as if he already knows the answer. Which he probably does because let's face it, he knows me better than I do most times.

"I'm getting there," I quietly admit.

"You freaking married this woman, yet you're only getting there?" Nash practically snarls as he takes a step toward me, shoving a finger in my direction. "You either are, or you aren't, man. Marriage isn't something to fuck around about."

"It's complicated," I mumble.

"Explain," he demands.

I've never seen my little brother act like this, so I wonder what else is going on. He's the most laid-back person I know, but the murderous look in his eyes has me immediately on the defense.

When he only stares, I come unleashed with emotion.

"You know as well as I do, I fucking love her, man. I have for months. But if I tell her something like that, she'll fucking run, and I'm scared as hell I'll lose her. I finally got her, and I'm not ready to let her go."

Blinking, he processes my words. "So... you said alcohol was involved; did you trick her into marriage?"

Shaking my head vehemently, I practically shout, "No. I swear. She made the decision on her own. But I did get a little spontaneous when it came to showing her how committed I am to her."

"Was she harboring feelings for you?"

That's a fair question, and I give him credit for asking.

"Yes. She actually admitted she almost didn't hire me because of her attraction."

"Does she love you?"

Again, a fair question, but one I don't know the answer to.

"There's the rub. I have no idea."

He's quiet for another long moment, then a slow smile spreads across his face. "I take it the chemistry is off the charts, or you wouldn't still be married."

There's no way I'm going into details with him, but I can't help but shake my head and laugh when memories of last night flash before me. "Uh... we broke her bed last night... and that's all you're getting from me."

"Holy shit. I think you're my hero," Nash whispers in awe.

"I married a woman on a whim, whom I have no idea if she loves me back, and I'm your hero? That makes zero sense."

"You fucking went for it, man. You laid it all on the line and had zero fucks to give for the consequences."

"Oh, I have all the fucks to give for the consequences," I counter. "If I fuck this up, I could lose everything. My job *and* the woman of my dreams."

"Oh, please, you can find a job anywhere—or hell, even venture out on your own. I know you have enough capital."

He's not wrong, but I have more to lose than my money. My heart is on the line, and I'm scared as hell I'll find a way to fuck this up. But I won't admit this to him.

"Okay, so you're married." He sighs as if he didn't just chew my ass five seconds ago. "Does this mean I finally get to meet the infamous Annabelle Holstings?"

"Yes, you'll get to meet her."

Slapping his hands together in glee, Nash rubs them as if he's plotting world domination. "Bring her to the next home game. It's an early game. We can come back here, and I'll order us dinner."

"That doesn't sound suspicious or anything," I tease. "But yeah, I'll bring her."

"Now that you're no longer single, will you still be able to help with the clinic this month?"

"Of course, I'll be there. If you're lucky, I'll even get Annie to help pass out snacks afterward."

Grinning, he asks, "It's Annie, is it? I can't wait to meet my new sister."

"For fuck's sake…" I mumble. "Let's get to work. I've got to get back to Seattle for my date tonight."

"Where are you taking her?" he asks with genuine interest.

"I've got a few ideas, but I need to get our meeting over with first. Now let's get to work, so I can spend the night with my wife."

"Love looks good on you, man," is the last he says about Annie until we're done with the planning for the next phase of our projects.

Then as I should've guessed, all bets are off. Nash is suddenly just as invested in me not fucking things up with her as he helps me plan an epic date.

Chapter 8

Nate

MY TONGUE STICKS to the roof of my mouth the moment Annie opens the door. She always looks nice, but today, she's wearing a royal-blue wrap dress I've never seen before. It hugs her body perfectly and makes her look like a total smoke show.

I can't deny it does feel good to have her peruse me over from head to toe, as if she's also been rendered speechless by my presence. I purposely wore the suit she's complimented me on before, and if the way she's licking her lower lip is any indication, I've met my mark.

Christ, if she doesn't stop looking at me like that, I'll scrap our plans for dinner and feast on her instead. Clearing my throat, I break our trance, and she blinks rapidly and shakes her head, as she rushes out, "Come in."

Leaning in to kiss her cheek, I ask, "Are you ready?"

Looking down at her bare feet, she rolls her eyes. "Sorry, got caught up at work. Wanna come upstairs while I finish getting ready?"

"You and I both know if I go anywhere near that bed upstairs, I'm gonna have my way with you. I'm here to take you on a proper date. So, I'll wait here, beautiful."

"Proper date? What are you, British?"

Geeze, if she only knew my thoughts right now.

"No... just a man doing everything he can to remain a gentleman." Remembering that I'm still holding the bouquet of roses I'd picked up along the way, I offer, "Want me to put these in water?"

Leaning in, she sniffs the roses. "These are beautiful. Thank you. If you don't mind, there's a vase under the sink. While you do that, I'll finish getting ready."

Without another word, she darts to her room, and I'm left tending to the flowers.

Of course, that doesn't take more than a few minutes, so I force myself to stay in the main living area. I busy myself by looking at the photos she has strung about her living room. I love that she has some of her grandma and a few of her, Teagan, and a boy I presume is Connor at the beach. They look so happy, enjoying themselves. I love seeing this side of her, the one that's carefree and living her life to the fullest.

She hasn't mentioned much about her family, but from my understanding, most of them live in Southern California, and she only sees them a few times a year, mostly at holidays. If we're gonna give this a go, I should probably find out more about them in the near future. I'm close to my family, so I can't imagine only seeing them sporadically.

The moment I hear her enter the room, I turn to greet her.

God, I'm a lucky bastard. I have no idea what I did to deserve this beautiful woman, but I'll take it.

Before my brain can process, my body's already in pursuit and stalking toward her. She looks good enough to eat, and I'd devour her in an instant. However, I must restrain myself if I truly want to make a point of spending time with her outside the bedroom and prove what we have is real.

When we're face-to-face, it takes all my self-control to simply lean in and whisper, "I've missed you," before claiming her lips.

As if I can't control myself, I grip the base of her neck and guide our kisses, so that I'm teetering on the edge of control. Knowing I need to stay on this side of the line, I reluctantly break our kiss, and my lips hover over hers as I remind both of us of my plans. "I've made reservations on the waterfront. We need to go if we're gonna make them."

Reaching for her hand, I grab the bag she's dropped beside us and lead her to the door.

"Always the gentleman," she teases.

"Trust me, my thoughts are nowhere near gentlemanly. Let's get out of here before I say to hell with it all and take you back to your room."

"Promises... promises."

This vixen may just be the death of me. But what a way to go.

"Oh, Annabelle, you have no idea what I want to do with you. But I'm determined to do this right..." I forcefully remind myself. "Let's go."

She quickly grabs her purse by the door, and I usher her through it, so I can lock up. Once we're in the car, she fills me in on the meeting with her lawyer, and we chat about our day.

I quickly find a place to park on the street, and we walk to the restaurant I've made reservations for. Just as we're about to enter, she gasps, "How'd you know?"

"I know a lot of things." I grin playfully. "You'll have to be more specific."

"Did you know this is my favorite restaurant?"

"I told you I pay attention. You talked about going here on your birthday last year with Teagan."

"That was like six months ago," she muses. "What else are you holding out on?"

Cocking a brow, I lean in and whisper so that only she can hear, "If I give away all my secrets, how will I keep you wanting more?"

She doesn't get the chance to respond because I give the hostess our name, and we're immediately ushered to a table with an incredible view of the water.

It's only a matter of minutes before drinks are ordered, we've perused the menu, and our selections are made. I suggest getting the sampler of sushi, with all of Annie's favorites included, as an appetizer as well as steaks for dinner. I'm starving, and I don't think sushi will fill me.

After the waiter leaves, Annie's expression turns unreadable as she stares in my direction. I've seen this look before, and I can only surmise that she's getting stuck in her head again. It's killing me, not knowing what has her wheels turning so hard, so I reach for her hand to give it a squeeze across the table.

"What are you thinking about so hard over there?"

"You," she admits with ease. "There's no sense in denying it. Just trying to process it all."

My laughter fills the space between us. "You and me both, beautiful," I tease. "But what has you so pensive all of a sudden?"

"I guess I'm wondering how this will all work. I mean... we work together, have two separate homes, and I'm sure you have an entire life I know nothing about. Normally, people have months or years to figure this out... and well... we jumped the gun and went straight to marriage. How the hell do I date my husband?"

"I'd sure like to figure that out," I say on a laugh. "But I'll make you a deal... let's start with keeping our communication open. I meant what I said before. Even though we're married, I still plan to date you regularly. I'm fairly certain we'll need to be intentional about this because life can easily get in the way."

"Nate, I barely have a life outside of work. How are you so certain we can do this?"

"Well, that's two separate issues," I pointedly remind her. "As far as work is concerned, I think you're gonna need to learn something you've yet to master—delegation."

Rolling her eyes, she sighs, "You make that sound so simple."

"First, I know you like things done *your* way, to which I honestly agree with ninety percent of the time, so it shouldn't be that difficult. But If I'm actually going to be your partner both in business and in life, you're going to need to talk to me. Let me know your needs, and I'll promise to do the same. You've spent years doing this on your own, and I've gotta say, I've got broad shoulders, and I can take some of the burden."

I watch carefully as she takes in my words and studies the grain of wood on the table. Then she glances at me from under her dark lashes and asks, "Would you be saying this if we weren't married?"

Would I? It's hard to separate my feelings from her.

A server brings us our drinks, and I take a moment to mull over my response. When we're finally alone, I admit, "Honestly, from a professional standpoint, I would expect that as your partner. You no longer need to be a one-woman show. I'm not just a partner for namesake. I want to grow and build Holstings' Creative just as much as you do. Your business plan makes sense, and it's an investment I'd make regardless of where we were personally."

"That's good to hear, but..." she trails off, then takes a sip of the white wine she's ordered. I wait patiently for her to continue.

Annie's usually extremely articulate and doesn't mince words, but this newfound situation we're in has her second-guessing a lot, and I don't blame her. I'm right there with her.

"Look," I finally say when the silence goes on for longer than I can handle. "I have no idea how to navigate this either, so you're not alone. But one thing I do know is I want to figure this out *together*. No one says we need all the answers today, right?"

A grin plays at her lips but never quite forms as she admits, "True. But there's still so much we don't know."

"Personally, I find that there's magic in the mystery. I love getting to know you... the real you, the side of you that you don't let most see. I love that I'm finding you're not the morning person I always believed you to be."

Her eyes widen in shock as her chin drops to her chest. "What's that supposed to mean?"

Chuckling, I think back to our morning. "Morning people don't need five alarms, Annie. You've always been bright eyed and bushy tailed each and every morning—no matter the time at the office. But I fucking love that you're human and are a bit groggy when you wake up. You swat at the alarm as if it's the most offensive thing, and you're not yourself until you've showered."

"How am I supposed to take that?"

Clearly, I've offended her, so I quickly back pedal. "*The point is*, without waking up with you, I wouldn't know this side of you. I wouldn't know that you ratchet the blankets, or that you love snuggling against my chest."

"Still, I'm not certain this is a good thing," she mutters adorably, and I want to kiss the pout right off her beautiful face.

"Okay, maybe not the best example, but the point I'm horribly trying to make is that I think if we knew everything about one another from the start, we'd be missing out on the exploration part of our relationship."

"I agree..." she draws out a sigh. "But you know me. I'm a planner... and well, I just didn't see you coming."

"No kidding." I laugh. "But in all fairness, I'm certain you wouldn't let yourself go there with me. Now that you have, is it still something you like?"

Shit. Why did I just lay myself out there like that?

"I think so, though the jury's still out. I hope you're not expecting a wife who cooks and keeps the house clean. Full disclosure, I'm only a functional cook at best, and I pay someone to clean my house once a week."

"First off, I want *you*—not a fictional character as my wife. I know firsthand, you have takeout more often than not; you're busy, and there's absolutely no shame in that. Second, this isn't the 1950s. I fully believe that as your partner in life, it's my responsibility to do my share as well. For the record, I happen to be a great cook, but like you, I hire someone to help maintain my house. God knows, I don't have the time for upkeep."

"Well, at least we can agree to that," she practically snorts. "Because time is something I don't have a lot of."

"What else can we cross off this list of worries you have?" I probe in wonder, while we wait for our food.

I can see her mentally tick through her list as I'm certain she has before settling on her most pressing issue. "Have you told your family about me?"

"Nash knows, and he's hoping you can make it to the clinic he's hosting this weekend to officially meet you in person."

"When is that again?"

"Well, if you're free, we'll go to the game Thursday night and to the clinic first thing Saturday morning."

"I think I can make that happen." She smiles. "But fair warning, I'm a pretty big fan of the Renegades. In fact, I often spend most of my Sundays at home on the couch with laptop in hand, watching them."

"I don't think you could be more right for me," I tease as

our food arrives to our table. "Though, I'm hoping I can convince you to see the home games in person."

"I think I might be persuaded."

"Great. I haven't missed one of Nash's home games yet, and I'd hate to start now. It's also a good thing I have two season tickets."

Her fork stops halfway to her mouth. "You know I'd never ask that of you, right? I mean, family is way too important."

I didn't think she would, but you never know.

"Speaking of family, do you miss not seeing yours?" I ask, completely changing the subject.

Slowly, she finishes the bite of steak she's chewing and exhales. "I miss my grandma the most. My parents... well... shit... how do I put this? Let's just say, I was a box they checked on their way up the corporate ladder."

What the fuck is she talking about? What the hell did they do to her? "Explain," I demand, so I don't voice my assumptions aloud.

"Dad's a corporate exec. He and Mom are more focused on climbing the social ladders than actually caring about being a family. They had me thinking it was a way to fit in with their peers at the time. They wanted the house, white picket fence, two point five children, etc. But when Mom discovered the ins and outs of parenting was extremely different from her expectations, she put an end to that and eventually filed for divorce. Having a kid meant she couldn't attend social functions for either of them. Thank God, Grandma didn't agree. I spent most of my summers and breaks with her and even convinced my parents to let me live with her for most of my junior and senior year."

"Are you kidding me?" slips out before I can stop myself.

Shaking her head, she shrugs. "Nope. It's part of the reason I'm so close to Teagan. We met when we were six and have been inseparable ever since. I spent most of my teenage years at her house or Grandma's."

"Holy shit. I had no idea."

"Yeah," she exhales heavily. "I don't talk about it much. It's also why I worked so freaking hard to do everything on my own. I didn't take a dime from my parents for my education or to start up my business."

"That's incredible," I say in awe. This woman is beyond words. The more I learn about her, the more I love.

Yeah. I went there. I've been falling for her for some time. But there isn't a doubt I don't love her. I just need to figure out a way to tell her, without freaking her out.

"I'm not sure I'd consider it incredible. But it's worked for me. I may not have student loans. But I'm mortgaged to the hilt."

"Stop downplaying your accomplishments or letting other people's opinions matter, Annabelle," I warn. "You're not even thirty, and you're running a successful company. That's a huge accomplishment in and of itself. You've made great friends, and I *personally* think you're pretty and damn awesome."

"Pretty and damn awesome... well, now I've heard it all." She laughs as she takes another bite of sushi.

"Nate... is that you?" I hear from across the room, and my jovial mood feels like a wet blanket has been thrown on it.

"I thought that was you," is much closer than I'd imagined, and I have no hopes of ignoring it.

Trying not to show my disappointment for my time with Annie being interrupted, I turn to face Ruby with a fake smile. "Hi, Ruby."

"Ohmigod," she gushes. "It's been ages." Leaning in, she hugs me tight as she kisses my cheek. "How are you doing?"

"I'm good." I shrug, hoping she'll get the hint that I'm not interested in conversation.

"Are you still working at Holstings' Creative?"

"Yep." I nod, giving a knowing smile to Annie.

Blowing out a heaving breath, Ruby shakes her head. "I still can't believe you took such a pay cut to work there. Did you end up remodeling your house like you'd planned, or did you have to put that off, too?"

The nerve of this woman.

Clearly, she has no idea who's sitting next to me.

"I finished the remodel early last year," I reply curtly, hoping she'll take the hint and leave.

Completely oblivious to the fact that I'm on a date, she gushes, "Oh, that's amazing. You'll have to invite me over, so I can check it out. I can't wait to see what you did with your bedroom."

The woman has the audacity to waggle her brows, and my fury builds instantly.

Before I can stop this, a woman's voice from behind us calls, "Ruby?" and motions for her to follow her toward a table.

Mussing my hair like a freaking five-year-old, she leans in and says, "Well, don't be a stranger, ya hear."

And with that, she walks off, leaving me feeling twitchy and my wife staring at me wide eyed and filled with questions.

Ah, fuck... how do I explain this?

Chapter 9

Annie

FROM THE MOMENT RUBY ARRIVED, Nate's entire demeanor changed. I watched the entire exchange feeling like a fly on the wall, since that woman literally paid me zero attention. Hell, I'm not even sure she was aware he was with anyone, as she only had eyes for him.

I vaguely remember someone working at Meyer & Cross who reminds me of her, but I can't be certain. She was on another team, and I had very little interaction with her. The woman I worked with was also a platinum blonde, not fiery red, so I can't be certain they are one and the same. But man, this woman is a piece of work.

"So..." Nate says on an exhale. "That was Ruby."

"I can see that," I say, crossing my arms in front of my chest as I lean back in my chair. Clearly, I need space, and this seating arrangement doesn't allow for much.

"Do you remember her from Meyer & Cross?" he asks, hesitation clear in his voice. After that awkward exchange, I can only imagine what he's going to say.

"I'm not sure that I do," I reply, fighting like hell to keep my expression neutral.

"When I first started working there, she and I dated a few times. Her sister is an interior designer, and she hooked me up with her to get my house decorated."

"Hooked you up," I say Clearly, he had something with her sister, too.

"Shit. That's not what I meant. You see, I bought a huge fixer-upper, and her sister was just starting out in the business. She and I worked a deal that she could use my home to build her portfolio, and I got to make my place look less like a bachelor pad. It was a win-win. Nothing nefarious. I swear."

"And why didn't Ruby see the finished product?" I probe, hoping he'll keep talking, and I won't have to ask more.

"Things with her... well, they didn't work out. I quickly learned she wasn't my type right after I started working with you and well... I moved on."

"How gracious of you. Did you move on with many others?"

Of course, my morbid curiosity got the best of me, but why the fuck did I just ask that? I seriously don't want to know the answer. Nate was the talk of the office at Meyer & Cross, and I'm certain he went out on his share of dates while we worked there.

He opens his mouth to talk, and I cut him off. "Wait. Don't answer that. I don't need to know this."

"It was about that time I realized that I only had eyes for you," he admits, and my mouth drops to the table.

"You dated plenty when you first started working for me," I hedge.

"I dated... yes... but nothing of any consequence... and

mostly to get my mind off you. After a while, going through the motions just didn't cut it for me, so I focused on work instead."

Wow. How do I even respond to that?

I mean, on one hand, he just admitted that he dated many women... on the other, he just verified that he was into me nearly a year ago. So, can I really be jealous of that?

"Look, I believe you. Why don't I take a trip to the ladies' room, and when I return, we can pretend Ruby never showed up? That sound good to you?"

Relief washes over Nate's face as he laughs. "Have I told you you're perfect for me?"

If only life could be so easy. The moment I walk out of the stall, I find Ruby with her ass propped up against the counter, waiting for me. She definitely has some stealthy stalker skills because I had no idea anyone was out here.

Doing my best to ignore her, I step up to the sink and wash my hands.

Of course, Ruby takes this time to look at herself in the mirror and reapply her red lipstick. When she's finished, she rubs her lips together with a smack. "I'd be careful if I were you."

Is she serious right now?

But I can't help myself, so I turn and challenge her in return. "Really? Why's that?"

"Nate may have mad skills in the sack, but he'll be a heavy hitter with your heart, so watch out."

Jesus. This woman is something else. "And what makes you the expert on all things Nate Bellinger?"

Fixing an out-of-place strand of hair from her bangs, she

nods to my reflection in the mirror. "We were pretty serious before he took that new job. I'd watch out if I were you."

Ohmigod, it's taking everything in my power to not smack the shit out of this pretentious bitch. But of course, I can't leave well enough alone. "And why's that?" I practically grit out, more out of morbid curiosity than rage at this point.

"First, Nate's a total workaholic. Once he started working at Holstings', I barely saw hide or hair from him. And second..." She pauses to turn in my direction to garner my full attention. "I'm fairly certain he's got a thing for his boss. He never shut up about her and if she ever called, he'd go running to help her. That woman has no respect for a man's personal time."

Holy shit. She did not just say that.

"Thank you for sharing." Reaching out my hand in her direction, I add, "I don't think we've had the pleasure of meeting. I'm Annabelle Holstings."

The look of pure shock on her face almost makes me break my composure and laugh. Her face morphs to almost ghostlike, as her eyes practically bug out of her head. I'm quite certain she's also swallowed her tongue because I swear it's nowhere to be seen in her mouth.

Somehow, without missing a beat, I continue, "I'm not only Nate's boss, but that sexy man out there is also my husband. I truly appreciate your concern to heed the warning. But I think I got it covered from here. Now..." I clap my hands and rub them together maniacally. "If you'll excuse me, I'm gonna take my husband home and fuck the ever-loving shit out of him."

Reaching for the door, I just can't leave well enough alone. "You have a good day now, ya hear."

Chapter 10

Annie

"YOU DID NOT ACTUALLY SAY that to her!" Nash practically shouts as I finish telling him about my encounter with Ruby in the bathroom.

We're having breakfast before the soccer clinic, and I've insisted we keep their tradition of meeting so they can discuss all the final details of the day. It's just a few blocks from the local high school where the clinic will take place. Nate assures me, no one recognizes Nash outside of his uniform, so it's fine to be this close.

"Yeah, she really did, Bro. I told you my wife is a total badass." Nate beams at me with pride as he squeezes my hand under the table.

Nash's eyes dart from me to Nate and back to me, while his jaw remains hanging like it's ready to fall off. "That's... well... that's diabolical. Holy shit. To be a fly on that wall." Shaking his head, he adds, "Remind me to never piss you off. You may be tiny in stature, but, man, you've got balls the size of Texas."

"I'm sure Ruby never saw it coming." Nate laughs. "Annie's a beast when she's taking care of business."

"I'm glad you think so highly of me." I laugh, rolling my eyes at their antics. I know it's a great story. Teagan nearly peed herself when I told her the next day. But I'm not as badass as they're making me out to be.

Nash pats Nate on the shoulder as his laughter continues. "I sure hope Annie made good on her promise that night." He laughs once again. "Ohmigod... fucking the ever-loving shit out of you... That's classic. You totally deserve that kind of fierceness, man."

"Oh, she rocks my world regularly," Nate admits. "But stop talking about my wife like that. As far as you're concerned—she's a goddess. She may be my sexual goddess, but as far as you're concerned, there's nothing sexual about her. Got it?"

"I hear ya loud and clear," Nash chortles. "Besides, she's the sister I never knew I needed. And I just can't think of her that way. It's weird."

I can't even with these guys. My cheeks hurt, and my stomach aches from the amount of laughter throughout breakfast. I swear, I haven't been able to keep a smile from my face from the moment Nash showed up with a baseball cap and dark sunglasses. Of course, Nate asked him who he was hiding from, and the constant ribbing continued from there.

When they're not pitching each other shit, the brothers effortlessly talk about the ins and outs of what to expect at today's clinic. My heart squeezes at their closeness. This is the type of family I always dreamed of having but never allowed myself to hope for. The only person I'm this in sync with is Teagan, but we have nothing on the Bellinger brothers.

Throughout breakfast, I glean more about my handsome

husband and his famous brother. My jaw dropped to the floor when I learned both Nate and Nash played soccer. Their dad was a huge fan and insisted the boys learn from the time they could walk. Apparently, they both played through high school and into college, though Nate stopped once he graduated. Nash, on the other hand, was recruited by the football team, played both sports through his junior and senior year, and was eventually drafted to play for the Rainier Renegades.

Another bit of information Nate had been holding out on is that the two of them have been running soccer clinics since Nash was in college. What started out as a way for Nash to earn some extra money during the off season became his passion project, and he created a foundation to help local youth in our surrounding area.

After hearing this, I finally break down and ask, "If you love soccer so much, Nash, why football?"

Chuckling, Nash shakes his head and shrugs. "It pays the bills."

"You're a professional kicker in the NFL simply because it pays the bills?" I ask incredulously.

Of course, Nate's quick to come to his brother's rescue. "He'd do camps for kickers on football teams, but there's not as much need for them. There are what?" He looks to Nash before finishing, "Only about thirty-two kickers in the entire NFL."

"Yep," Nash agrees. "Soccer's a bigger bang for my buck, if I want to share my passion for footwork with our local youth."

Seeing the conviction in his eyes, I sigh, "You really are incredible, Nash."

"Hey, now." Nate's chest puffs out, pretending to be bothered by my compliment.

Swatting at Nate, I roll my eyes and return my attention to Nash. "I love that you're letting me be even a small part of this. I've always wanted to find a way to be a bigger part of our community. Thanks again for including me in this today."

When we arrive at the field, I immediately get put to work with the volunteers to help check in the kids. Since they're due to arrive soon, I'm briefly given a crash course orientation by the lead volunteer in this area.

I watch from afar how Nash and Nate work with a host of other volunteers to set up stations around the entire stadium. Some will be running sprints and doing conditioning along the track, others a series of drills, and the rest will be at various stations created to increase their endurance and enhance their agility.

Once we get everyone checked in, I volunteer to help set up the snack station for when the time comes. It also allows me to watch the players in action. Nash has managed to get about twenty-five college players to volunteer their time along with coaches they have permanently on staff to run the clinics.

No matter what I'm doing, my eyes never stray far from Nate. It's as if my body senses his every movement and all it takes is to look up, and I can easily track him around the stadium. Watching him demonstrate skills, coach kids through the movements, and encourage them as they try their best to mimic him is endearing. My heart melts each time he high-fives or fist bumps a player.

By the time the kids are ready for a break, their snacks are ready. I've helped assemble bags with fruit, crackers, protein bars, and trail mix. Each player also gets to pick out their favorite sports drink from the chest of coolers lined up around the tables.

If they walk away hungry, it's on them. Nash's catering a full lunch for the families as well when it's over, so their siblings and parents can visit with coaches. I never knew so much went into running a camp in my life. But it makes me proud to be just a small part of it. Next time, I'll use some of my strings to help garner donations to offset the costs as well.

I'm restocking the table with bags from underneath when I feel Nate's presence. The hairs on the back of my neck prickle as shivers race throughout my body before I look up and see him. Even though it's a cool autumn day, heat rushes through me, when he slides a hand along my back as I stand. I'm dressed in workout clothes, leggings, a tank, and a thin hoodie, but I may as well be naked by how my body reacts to this man.

"Hey, you," he whispers, leaning in to kiss my cheek. "Having fun?"

"Absolutely. I've got so many ideas for who I can reach out to as potential sponsors in the future. I'm totally hitting up our clients before the next clinic. Fair warning. This is such an amazing cause."

"You better look out, Nate. She's gonna take over your job in a heartbeat," Nash teases as he joins us.

"As long as it stays in the family, I'm sure we can figure it out." Nate shrugs as he wraps an arm around me. "We're just lucky she likes it, or you'd be out on your ear."

"Oh, please..." I groan, swatting at his chest in clear

disapproval. There's no way I'd ever come between Nate and his brother. Between grabbing drinks after the football game earlier this week and breakfast this morning, I know their bond is something I'd never interfere with. I could only wish to have a family as supportive as his.

Suddenly, I'm sandwiched between the two of them, and both sling their arms around me as Nash leans in to kiss my cheek. "I knew there was a reason I liked you."

"Hey, now, get your own wife," Nate teases.

"Why, yours is so cute and perfect..." When Nate levels him with a glare, Nash quickly tacks on, "For you, bro. She's perfect for you."

Letting go of me, he steps aside. "Besides, I've got my eyes on someone else."

Nate's eyes widen and look around. "Really? Why is this the first I've heard of this mystery woman?"

Nash rolls his eyes and shakes his shoulders. "Because it's complicated. But if anything comes of it, I promise you'll be the first to know. In the meantime, it's too much fun keeping you on your toes with Annie."

Now it's my turn to protest. "Hey, now, I'm happily married to the man I never knew I could wish for."

"Can you say that louder, for those in the back?" Nate grins, pulling me close.

I feel a soft kiss at my temple as he squeezes me tight.

Later that night, while we're snuggled in bed, and he's tracing imaginary circles along my spine, Nate catches me off guard when he asks, "Did you mean it?"

"Mean what?" I ask groggily. We've just made love, and

I'm in that state of post-orgasmic bliss that I never want to leave. My body is in the perfect Jell-O-like state, and I'm snuggled up to my husband.

He clears his throat and clarifies, "What you said to Nash... about being happily married?"

Chapter 11

Nate

SITTING UP, Annie repositions herself to look me in the eye. I stare at her for the longest time, barely able to breathe before she finally puts me out of my misery and whispers, "Yeah. I meant it."

Needing us to be on the same page, I press her further, "But we don't have all the details worked out yet, and you're a stickler for the details."

Sighing heavily, she grins. "That was before you barged your way into my life and made it impossible to live without you."

"Speaking of living with me... what would you say to us living here? Not only is my place bigger, but it's closer to work. And... it comes furnished with a king-size bed and that sunk-in tub you seem to enjoy."

"But would you be okay with me moving all my crap in here? You'd have to share that beautiful walk-in closet with my haphazard organization."

It's true; it bugs the crap out of me that she *never* has her closet organized. She literally just hangs things at random in the dry-cleaning bags, keeps her clothes in a laundry basket until she needs them again, among many other things I've learned about her these past few weeks. Don't even get me started on the amount of space she uses on the bathroom counter. But I'll take her and her dry cleaning if it means waking up each morning with her in my arms.

"I think I can handle it," I tease, leaning in to kiss her.

When we break apart, she runs her hands through my hair as she admits, "Honestly, Nate, I don't care where we live as long as I'm with you. I have no idea how you did it, but you've completely wormed your way into my heart. You've somehow, without knowing, given me a sense of home and the family I never knew I was missing. I love you, Nate Bellinger, and my home is where you are."

All the breath leaves my chest as she makes her declaration. I'm left staring at her breathless and in awe. I don't think I'll ever forget this moment in my life. Knowing Annabelle Holstings loves me is the best feeling in the world.

When my brain finally catches up with my heart, I palm her cheek and run my thumb along her lips. "I'm fairly certain I love you more," I whisper before hauling her up my body and kissing her.

Our bodies move in sync as our hearts soar. Before I know it, we're making love all over again. We repeat the words *I love you* over and over as we devour one another. When I finally enter her, I give her my heart, body, and soul completely. Annabelle Holstings is it for me and now that she's finally admitted she feels the same, I vow, I'm never letting her go.

Epilogue

Nate

Eight months later

IT'S BEEN all hands on deck for the past few weeks as we put together the final touches for the Worthington account. Annie and I have been to Vegas several times, each time taking an extra day to see her grandma Pauline in Palm Springs.

It has been amazing getting to know the person who essentially raised the woman I've grown to love more each day. It's important to both Annie and me to have the people who mattered most here for the opening of The Worthington. So, we've arranged for Pauline, my parents, and brother to join us in celebration. This is a grand opening like no other, and I can't be happier with the results of our efforts.

The ribbon-cutting ceremony is due to start any moment, and I can't help but smile because Annie and I have actually pulled this project off. We've helped get this place booked to nearly full capacity, and the lobby looks better than either of us could've imagined. Our employees have worked their asses off, and we deserve a vacation after months of non-stop working.

Annie holds my hand as we listen to Mr. Worthington welcome everyone with his speech. For a multi-billionaire, he's one of the most down-to-earth people I know. We've met with him several times over these past few months to ensure his vision is brought to life.

"And now… please help me express my gratitude and appreciate the efforts of those who made this night happen. I'm happy to introduce the founder of Holstings' Creative. Ms. Holstings, would you like to say a few words?"

I squeeze Annie's hand once before she leaves to step up to the podium. "Thank you, Mr. Worthington, for allowing Holstings' Creative to be a part of your plan for this event. I would like to make one correction though."

The entire room pauses, and I'm even waiting on bated breath to wonder what would possibly be wrong.

Reaching out her hand in a silent plea for me to join her, she starts again, "If you'll allow me a personal point of privilege, Mr. Worthington, I'd like to introduce my team. First, I want to start off by saying my name's no longer Annabelle Holstings. It's Annabelle Bellinger. I'm the founder of Holstings' Creative, but I'm just one small piece of this team. Thanks to you and this project, Mr. Worthington, I've come to realize that my partner, Nate Bellinger, is more than just a colleague. In fact, it was our pitch for this very company that brought us together as husband and wife. For that, I am forever grateful we were brought here for our Vegas Pitch to you. Mr. Worthington, thank you for taking a chance on us as a team. You have no idea how life changing this opportunity became. We look forward to working with you again in the future."

With that, she hands the microphone back to Mr.

Worthington, and he proceeds with the ribbon-cutting ceremony. But I'm still replaying Annie's words in my mind.

Once the ribbon's been cut, Annie pulls me aside from the crowd and asks, "What's going on, Nate?"

"Did you just proclaim in front of everyone that you've changed your last name?"

Waggling her brows, she tips up on her toes and whispers, "You caught that, did you? You have no idea the amount of paperwork it takes, but it became official last week. However, I wanted to wait until Vegas to share the news with you. After all, it only seemed appropriate. I'm so glad that what happened in Vegas didn't stay here. I love you, Nate Bellinger, and I can't imagine my life without you."

Wrapping my arms around her, I stop, just before my lips crash onto hers, to test it out for myself. "And I love you more than life itself, *Mrs. Bellinger.*"

The End

THANK you for taking a chance on **The Vegas Pitch**. There are so many books you can choose from, and I'm honored you've chosen to read mine. If you're interested in hearing how Teagan and Davis came together, their story is complete and ready to read in **He Saved My Boy.**

For those of you interested in Nash Bellinger, don't worry. He'll be getting his own story in the next installment of the

Rainier Renegades series, ***Making the Kick***. Be sure to sign up for my newsletter to stay up to date and be notified when it becomes available.

To be notified when Making the Kick is available, be sure to join Amanda Shelley's Newsletter to stay up to date with all her releases. https://geni.us/ZanderNL

You can also check out her books here: https://geni.us/AmandaShelleyBooks

ABOUT THE AUTHOR

Amanda Shelley writes romantic stories you can escape into. Some are steamy, others are sweet but all have strong characters with a little bit of sass.

When not writing, Amanda enjoys time with her family, playing chauffeur, chef and being an enthusiastic fan for her children. Keeping up with them keeps her alert and grounded in reality. She enjoys long car rides, chai lattes and popping her SUV into four-wheel drive for adventures anywhere.

Amanda loves hearing from readers. Be sure to sign up for her newsletter and follow her on social media. Join her reader's group Amanda's Army of Readers to stay up to date on her latest information.

Readers group: https://www.facebook.com/groups/Amandas ArmyofReaders/

Goodreads: https://www.goodreads.com/author/show/
19713563.Amanda_Shelley
Newsletter: https://geni.us/AmandaShelleyNL
www.amandashelley.com

ACKNOWLEDGMENTS

First, I would like to thank you the reader, blogger, and reviewer for taking the time to read this book. There are so many stories to choose from, and I'm humbly honored you've chosen to read mine. I hope you enjoyed Annie and Nate's story. I'd love to hear from you and your thoughts about The Vegas Pitch. You can find me on social media, my reader's group *Amanda's Army of Readers*, or at www.amandashel ley.com. If you care to share your thoughts on this book with other book lovers, please consider leaving a review at any of the retail sites or on Goodreads, BingeBooks, and BookBub.

Next, I'd like to thank S.L. Sterling for creating the Hot Vegas Nights Series. Not only is she an incredible person to work with, but she is an incredible designer. I absolutely love what you did for the cover of this book as well as the entire series. Without you, The Vegas Pitch would have never happened. Thanks so much for taking a chance on me and bringing me into this world. I've enjoyed working with the authors who've collaborated in this series as well.

This book wouldn't be what it is without my amazing team of support. To Renita McKinney at A Book A Day Author Services, thank you for helping me develop Annie and Nate's characters and make them into the best they can be. Thanks so much for having my back and making this happen.

To Sue Soares, thank you for your continued support in helping me make my writing the best it can be. I look forward to working with you on many books to come.

To Julie Deaton at Deaton Author Services, thanks for making my book pretty and talking me off a ledge. I appreciate knowing your proofreading is exquisite, and my worries disappear. Your eagle eyes are spectacular, and I don't know what I'd do without you. I absolutely love your notes and look forward to your reactions.

To the people who have supported me along the way, I'm humbly grateful to have you in my life. Whether you've read my books, asked me about my progress, listened to me talk about my fictional characters as if they're a part of my family, plotted with me, or been my cheerleader, I appreciate your continued support. Please know it hasn't gone unnoticed.

Last but certainly not least, to my four beautiful girls who have had to wait patiently when I said, "Just one more minute," when I obviously meant a lot more than one. I love that you get that I have deadlines and will sometimes keep me on task with your not-so-subtle reminders that "Mom... you should be working" during my designated times. I appreciate your support more than you'll ever know. Even though you can't read this book—because that might be *weird*—for both of us, I love that you keep asking. I love you all more than words can express. You're the reason I continue to strive and reach for my goals each day.

If you enjoyed this book, you will be happy to discover Amanda Shelley primarily writes in one world. For a complete list of the series reading order as well as a chronological time line, please visit:

https://amandashelley.com/reading-order/

Zander: A Perfectly Independent Series Novella

(FREE ON ALL RETAILERS)

Zander's known for being a player both on and off the court.

When his name shows up as my next client, my heart stalls, and not in a good way. There's no way I'll survive the semester with him. I just don't have the patience.

However, when I need help, Zander makes a proposal I can't refuse. He'll be my fake date to my best friend's wedding so I don't have to face my ex and his new girlfriend alone.

The weekend goes off without a hitch as we effortlessly pretend to have the time of our lives.

All is perfect... until I realize my feelings for Zander are no longer an act.

What will I do when our arrangement comes to an end?

Drew: Book One of the Perfectly Independent Series

Of all people, why him?

He didn't EVEN bother introducing himself, just assumed I knew him from his fame on the court.

I nearly died on the spot when our professor announced we were permanent lab partners. Between his arrogance and the constant interruption from basketball groupies, there's no way I'll survive this semester.

Sure, he's hotter than anyone I've ever seen in a science lab with his sexy blue eyes, cute dimple, and muscles for days - but I can't afford *his* kind of distractions.

Okay. Deep breath.

I can do this.

After all, it's only one semester.

Just when I think my self-control is in check, he does something to show me that he isn't the egotistical, self-centered jerk I thought he was.

How can his stupid smile suddenly make my mind melt, heart race, and palms sweat?

If I take this chance on Drew, will my perfectly laid out plans disappear?

https://geni.us/AmandaShelleyBooks

Vince: Book Two of the Perfectly Independent Series

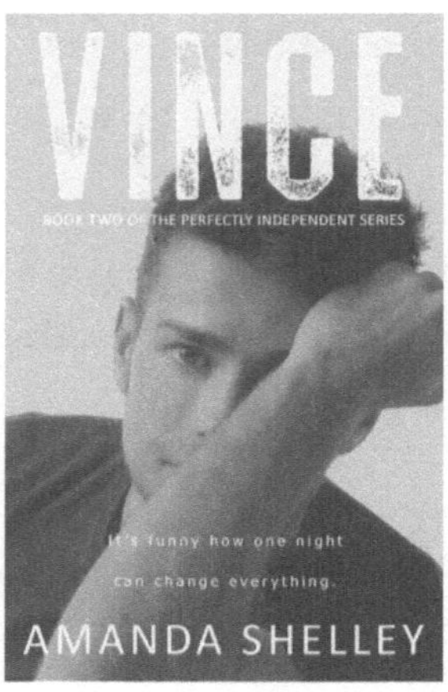

It's funny how one night can change everything.

As a bartender near campus, I'm certain I've heard it all. Rarely a shift passes without some guy taking his best shot, hoping I'll end my self-proclaimed dating diet.

Of course, this is exactly how I meet Vince.

Except, he isn't the one running his mouth.

No, he simply shuts down his idiotic friend, then stops my heart with the simplest of smiles and walks away.

Just when I force myself to forget him, he bumps into me on campus.

Our connection is consuming, and my world is knocked off kilter. It's far beyond physical attraction. He's smart, sexy, and feels like—home?

Wait, that can't be right...

Whatever it is, Vince has me breaking my rules to spend time with him.

My entire life I've prepared for meeting the wrong guys.

What the hell should I do when I find the right one?

https://geni.us/AmandaShelleyBooks

Damien: Book Three of the Perfectly Independent Series

Beautiful girls are not hard to find at Columbia River University.

The coeds on campus are great to look at but I was over that scene after graduation three years ago.

These days, outside of being part of the largest civil engineering job on campus, all I'm searching for is a decent meal and some peace and quiet. It's why I'm happy to have found what I consider a hidden gem in the diner I frequent.

All I need to do is finish this job and move on to the next by year's end.

Should be easy enough. Only when Vanessa walks up with a sexy smile and a mouth full of sass, she does more than take my order. She completely takes my breath away.

Next thing I know, I'm here every morning, making every excuse to dine with this intriguing woman. Not only is she smart and sexy, but she's laser focused on reaching the goals she's set for herself.

The more I get to know her, the more I'm convinced she's the one. I just have to find a way to get her to deviate from her perfectly laid plans and take a chance on me.

https://geni.us/AmandaShelleyBooks

Making The Call

Dani

As a bestselling romance author, most assume my life's glamorous, filled with combustible chemistry, and most of all, romance. Ha! I can only wish. With a deadline looming, I've escaped to my family's cabin on Anderson Island to free myself from distractions. My plan's great, until a man, who could pass as a cover model on one of my books, comes to my rescue. Is there chemistry? Sure. Is he everything I'd look for in a guy? Absolutely. But will my career be at risk if I give into my desire?

Luke

For a player, women line up outside the locker room. For coaches, we're lucky to get in the game. As the youngest NFL coach in the league, I live, eat, breathe, and even sleep football. To gear up for this season, I return to my home on Anderson Island for a much-needed break. When Dani literally crashes into my life, my mind's suddenly on the sexy brunette with a sailors mouth, rather than my team's next play. She has me dusting off another playbook entirely, making me wonder, did I make the right call?

https://geni.us/AmandaShelleyBooks

The Summer Dare

Leave it to Nana to think of everything.

After a grueling semester, I'm ready for a peaceful summer in Seaside with my sisters.

Imagine my surprise, when I'm woken by the screeching sound of a saw coming through my wall, the first official morning of break.

Not only did I come flying out of bed swinging, but I gave Ryan, the unsuspecting carpenter the surprise of his life, when I came wielding my killer coat hanger and all.

Too bad, I was only in a tank and undies and it wasn't nearly as effective as I'd hoped.

Of course, he insists he's only doing his job. Since it's Nana's last request to care for us, I can't refuse.

However, I won't let a tall, pesky, sexy as sin, know-it-all get in my way of my summer plans. I pretend I ignore him – that is until my youngest sister pokes her nose in my business and throws down a dare I can't back down from.

Kiss the next single guy who walks up to the bonfire – or explain to my sisters why I get riled up over the contractor.

When Ryan suddenly appears, I know I'm screwed in more ways than one.

Not only will my sisters learn my secret, but from the determined look on Ryan's face, I'm afraid he's eager to reveal it to the world as well.

What have I gotten myself into?

As I walk toward him, one thing is certain – this summer dare will either make or break me.

https://geni.us/AmandaShelleyBooks

The Summer Ultimatum

Watching my sister fall in love last summer gave me something I hadn't expected—hope.

It gave me hope that there might be someone out there for me and hope that I might get past my misguided fears and finally let someone in.

With my help, Ryan's planning the most epic proposal. I just have to get the know-it-all musician I work with to fall in line to make it work.

Jax is wicked smart, extremely talented, and sexy as sin. But he can't see the forest for the trees when it comes to his potential. He'd rather keep playing in dive bars along the coast than take a real shot at success.

When the Seaside festival has a music competition, I present Jax with an ultimatum that will either make or break both our careers.

I've laid it all on the line, but can he?

https://geni.us/AmandaShelleyBooks

The Summer Proposal

My sisters are dropping like flies.

They're falling in love and having the time of their lives.

Don't get me wrong, I'm ecstatic for them. I love seeing them happy.

But I'm not ready for that type of commitment.

I can't even keep a plant alive, let alone find someone worthy of getting past a third date.

As the only sister done with school and single as a pringle, I have to do something fast, or I'll be my matchmaking aunt's next victim.

When Jax's drummer joins him for the summer and needs some help with his image, I make him a deal he can't refuse.

All is perfect—until I realize my summer proposal has one minor flaw.

Our relationship may be a sham, but there's nothing fake about my feelings for Finn.

https://geni.us/AmandaShelleyBooks

The Summer Arrangement

One, two, three—it's all down to me.

As the youngest and only single Lancaster, I'm eager to spend my summer in Seaside, Oregon, with my sisters. It's something I've looked forward to all year, and I'm determined to make every minute count. After all, I've only got one year before I graduate from college and have to adult for real.

However, if I want to graduate debt free, I need to work. I have a lead on the perfect summer job with the nanny agency I've spent the last three summers catering to.

I just have to win over an adorable three-year-old and convince her single dad I'm the right one for the job.

Simple enough, right?

Except when I show up at his door, I'm shocked to find he's the guy I hooked up with a few times last semester.

This cannot be happening.

I need this job. There's too much on the line to walk away.

Maybe we can put the past behind us and make some sort of summer arrangement?

https://geni.us/AmandaShelleyBooks

The Summer I Found Home

Being a pilot is all I've ever known.

I served my country and I'm damn proud of my career.

But sacrifices were made, especially when it came to family.

I've missed first steps, first days of school, and first dates to name a few.

My kids grew up. They're having families of their own.

Was it worth it?

When an opportunity brings me to Seaside, I jump feet first no questions asked.

It means experiencing all those firsts with my grandkids.

With family as my focus and my guard down, I don't even see Faye coming.

She's a force to be reckoned with and has me holding on for dear life.

I thought our ship had sailed, but now that I'm home for good—*I just might get more than one second chance.*

arrangement?

https://geni.us/AmandaShelleyBooks

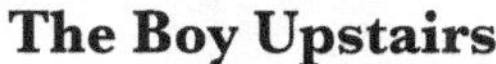

The Boy Upstairs

I ran into Derek while trying to escape the neighbor from hell.

Instantly, we hit it off. Since he's only here for three months and the microbrewery leaves me little time for commitments, it's the perfect setup for a fling.

He's adventurous, challenges me, and he just gets me from the inside out.

With our expiration date quickly approaching, I'm left to wonder... *Will my heart ever be the same without the boy upstairs?*

https://geni.us/AmandaShelleyBooks

He Saved My Boy

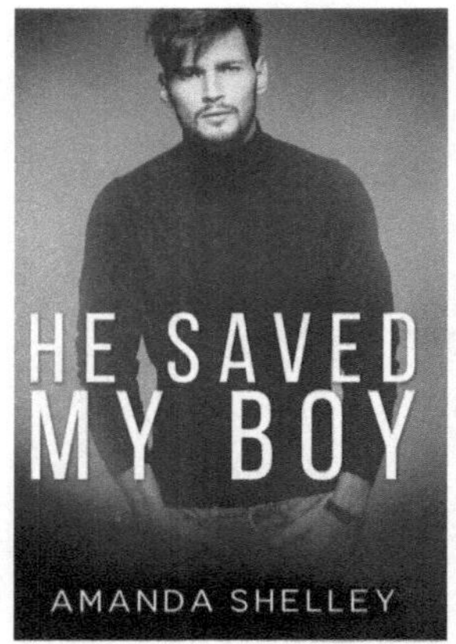

Davis is the first guy to catch my attention since... hell, I don't even know.

Instantly, he makes me think and feel things I've forgotten existed. It has been forever since I put my needs first, so I take the chance and let him light me up from the inside out.

Our night is the kind that will ruin me for all others.

But then I get the dreaded call.

I rush out without a second glance, knowing I'll likely never see him again.

My son will always come first—Always.

Imagine my surprise when Davis walks in, and I find he's the only one who can save my boy.

This cannot be happening—*I guess it's time to pull up my big girl panties and see what happens.*

https://geni.us/AmandaShelleyBooks

Resilience: Book One of Resilience Duet

Resolution: Book Two of Resilience Duet

Samantha never saw Enzo coming.

As the dust settles from her divorce, her life is full. She doesn't have time for distractions. She's too busy running her own company and checking off numerous items from her kids' demanding schedule to have a life of her own.

Then he walks into her kitchen with his breathtaking green eyes and a mischievous grin. He's there to surprise his father - her contractor, but his presence makes everything off kilter.

Enzo's perfectly content with his adventurous life as an elite rescue pilot, until a harmless prank turns on him. Instead of surprising his father, he finds his world thrown off course by the beautiful woman with a sexy smile, wicked sass and the mouthwatering ability to keep him on his toes.

With his limited time on leave, is she worth the risk to his heart?

https://geni.us/AmandaShelleyBooks

Collide: A Sweet Romance

Falling head over heels was the last thing I expected.

Literally.

Coffee is everywhere – and more than my ego is bruised.

When the handsome stranger I plowed into calls me by name, mortification sinks in.

He rushes off to class. I run home to change, hoping to forget the whole incident.

If only I could be so lucky.

I quickly find it's a small world and Gavin Wallace is completely unavoidable. Everywhere I turn he's there. In my classes. Hanging with my friends.

I've got his full attention and I have to admit, I like it a lot more than I should.

https://geni.us/AmandaShelleyBooks

9 781951 947507